Winner of the
Drue Heinz Literature Prize
1990

RICK HILLIS

UNIVERSITY OF PITTSBURGH PRESS

Published by the University of Pittsburgh Press, Pittsburgh, Pa. 15260

Copyright © 1990, Rick Hillis

All rights reserved

Baker & Taylor International, London

Manufactured in the United States of America

Library of Congress Cataloging-in-Publication Data

Hillis, Rick, 1956–
    Limbo river / Rick Hillis.
        p.   cm.
    "Winner of the Drue Heinz literature prize, 1990"—P.
    ISBN 0-8229-3653-4
    I. Title. II. Title: Drue Heinz literature prize, 1990.
    PR9199.3.H4853L56 1990
    813' .54—dc20   90-33963

The author wishes to express his gratitude to the Saskatchewan Arts Board, the Canada Council, the Canada Council Explorations Program, and Stanford University for support during the writing of this book; also the Banff Centre for the Arts, the Yaddo Foundation, and the Saskatchewan Artists Colonies where many of these stories were written.

The portion of the song which appears on page 123 is from "Donald and Lydia," written by John Prine, © 1971, WALDEN MUSIC, INC. & SOUR GRAPES MUSIC. All rights administered by WB MUSIC CORP. All rights reserved. Used by Permission.

"Blue" and "Limbo River" originally appeared in *Prism International;* "Betty Lou's Getting Out Tonight" was first published in *Descant;* "Summer Tragedy Report" first appeared in *Grain;* "The Eye" is reprinted from *The Coe Review;* "Eagle Flies on Friday; Greyhound Runs at Dawn" and "Rumors of Foot" were originally published in *Canadian Fiction Magazine.*

Some of these stories also appeared in the following anthologies: *The Old Dance* (Coteau Books), *Sky High: Stories from Saskatchewan* (Coteau Books), *The Last Map Is the Heart* (Thistledown Press). "The Storyteller" was originally printed in *87: Best Canadian Stories* (Oberon) and "Betty Lou's Getting Out Tonight," "Summer Tragedy Report," and "Rumors of Foot" appeared in *Coming Attractions 6* (Oberon). The stories "Blue" and "The Storyteller" were broadcast on CBC radio.

To Patsy
and Big Ben

CONTENTS

LIMBO RIVER

$\mathcal{B}$LUE

Lubnickie slams the truck door and leans up the ramp to the shop. Nothing new about that, but this morning Murdoch grabs his arm as soon as he steps inside, gives him a shake, gets his goddamn attention.

"You seen them yet?"

"Don't even think like that," says Lubnickie.

But when his eyes get used to the dark and he sees them, it's true. Three of them, two in their early twenties with faces like they got off at the wrong bus stop, the other one older, maybe thirty or so, and hard looking. She's got on men's jeans and dirty running shoes with the toes worn through on top. Her hair is reddish, tied from her face with a green scarf. One of the younger ones has on dress shoes with pointed heels and keeps lifting her feet one at a time like a flamingo. The other young one glances at the men lining the cement walls. When she gets to Lubnickie she crosses her arms and sits on a dope pail with her knees pinched.

The door from the front offices swings open and Finch comes in, his Hushpuppies scratching on the slagged cement. He has a clipboard and is flipping through some sheets of paper.

"As you can tell, we have some new faces this morning," he says from the middle of the shop. "I know you'll make them welcome." He starts to list which woman goes on which crew when Lubnickie clanks his steel thermos against the wall. Finch looks up from his clipboard.

"Eddy?"

Lubnickie's mouth feels like springs are snapping it around.

"I told you before I don't work with a woman," he says. All

the men are looking at him funny and his voice is shaking. "I'll wobble before I work with a dame."

"*Ed!*" Finch holds out a hand like he's checking for spit.

"I got nothing against them, but *Jesus Christ,* this used to be a production outfit. I'll go back to work on the Alaska big inch before I work with a honey."

"Right on, Ed," Finch mumbles, "but—"

Lubnickie looks at the knots of men. How would they like their wives or daughters up to their asses in mud and grease? "Maybe some of you don't know what happened the time they tried to put women to work on the big inch up north," he says to them. "Ask Finch about it sometime."

One of the younger girls makes a windy sound like she's going to cry, and Lubnickie swears.

Then the only sound is his boot heels clicking down the ramp across the tarmac. He gets in his half ton, watches the dark maw of the shop for movement.

Lubnickie recalls the old days. Huge union meetings with everybody in good clothes and matching ball jackets, pounding their fists, standing up for what was right. He envisions a wobble, probably violent. There would be TV coverage. He sees a blurred image of himself on the six o'clock news. Blurred because he is flinging himself in front of the wheels of a scab-operated truck. Placards are waving. A woman reporter wades into the horde of blue collars, and the strikers scream into her microphone like wrestlers do. He is interviewed in the TV van and tells the story of up north when a woman who could hardly drive a car was operating the boom that cradled the pipe, how she let the pipe fall and how the man—a personal friend from Moose Jaw, Saskatchewan—lost his leg. Sure, accidents happened in this line of work, but come on.

Lubnickie waits for the exodus of lunch-kit-swinging men. Any second now. But when a few trickle out, it's only to smoke. They make a point of not looking at Lubnickie's truck.

Ok. Lubnickie cranks the ignition, rattles the gear shift back and forth across neutral. Where the hell are the old hands at least? What's going on? The machinery parked in the chained-off compound look like markers in a graveyard, costing money. The men aren't moving. Suddenly Lubnickie gets it. They are waiting for him to leave. He jams the gearshift and the tires scream, leave part of themselves on the ground.

Norma, the older of the women, fixes her eyes on a spot on the wall where no one is leaning. She is nervous, more frightened than she would ever admit, especially to herself. But seeing these cocky men with their pressed blue jeans and polished boots makes her think *screw everybody*. Screw the younger ones with their muscle cars and designer jeans that cost more than the parka she's worn through at the elbows. Screw the older guys with their grade eight educations, permanence, colored TVs, second cars, houses with nice lawns, big weddings for their daughters, holidays in the summer. She knows who they are because she's seen their wives in the mall, spending money their husbands made, dressing like the catalogue. And screw, she thinks, her old man Colin, home right now in bed probably, who could have been one of these men except for the booze and temper that made him walk off jobs when things got bad. Screw the whole kit and caboodle for making people want what they saw on TV and not giving them the means to get even what they need.

Norma hates these guys. The one called Finch and the redneck Eddy. They make fifteen bucks an hour and welfare pays her three hundred and fifty a month. She's supposed to feed and clothe two kids on this, yet. This is her chance, nobody's taking it away. She thinks of last night, nervous about the job, cranking tobacco filter tubes at the kitchen table. Her two kids, Terry and Tracy, watching TV, eating a whole box of Ritz. Tracy, her fourteen year old, copping the odd cigarette before Norma can put them in the Tupperware case. Colin coming home stoned and sad. He can't find a job because of the times and because nobody wants a thirty-eight-year-old laborer on the payroll, and now he can't afford to license his Harley.

"I don't want my woman working on the pipeline," he said. "Don't do this to me, honey."

It was strange to see him sad like that, with his face in his hands at the kitchen table.

"Somebody changed the rules on me and I don't know what to do," he said. He was referring, Norma knew, to the poster she found at the welfare office: Blue Women Wanted. A work project created to expose women to the trades; to share a bit of the grant money the government paid to construction. She told Colin about it, but welfare dads weren't wanted. The only work for them was sporadic labor from Temporary Manpower if you could get down there early enough in the morning. Unloading semis and whatnot. Colin was too old to be doing that.

When Lubnickie walked away, Norma thought of Colin. How much they were probably the same, but how things had made them different.

Myrtle Lubnickie is kneading bread dough with blue-veined fists. She sees her husband's rig pull into the driveway and looks over at the clock. She is wearing her checkered apron with the big patch pockets and frills. A cigarette is going in the ashtray. It's eight o'clock in the morning.

Myrtle wonders why Ed doesn't get out of the truck. The sun is shining right in his windshield, and he just sits there, head resting on the steering wheel. Myrtle marvels at how she both understands Ed and still doesn't even after all these years. He's the type of man who will stay where he is if he wants to. He won't want to talk about it and Myrtle won't ask. He's her Ed. He has been ever since his crew came into her community when they were both teenagers, and he stole her away from the poverty of her parents' farm where she only had one nice outfit and had to wear red rubber boots for dress.

Myrtle has been up since before Ed. She'd made his eggs and coffee. Now she is making bread and buns because a home needs these. She may make pies as well, pumpkin and chocolate, because Ed likes pie. At ten o'clock she will cross the street to coffee with Carol and smoke several cigarettes. Or Carol may coffee here since the bread will be rising. Carol's husband is a schoolteacher, but Carol is pretty down-to-earth despite this. Myrtle likes it when she and Ed hobnob with intelligent people even though she believes she is too stupid to truly comprehend what anybody is talking about. She doesn't care because her life is what she wants. A nice home with a dishwasher, plenty of money for groceries if nothing else, a small, beat-up Mazda for her to scoot around in, a healthy routine. In the afternoon

Myrtle will erect the ironing board in front of the TV and watch her soaps. She does Ed's clothes by heart. It's routine now. Everything blue, nicely faded.

Lubnickie dismounts his truck and circles behind it. The box has been transformed into his welding rig, a rack of metal he and Murdoch put together last winter. It is full of nooks for pipe fittings, cutting oil, thread dope, welding rods, tools, gray paint, his stinger, mask, cutting apparatus. It is a source of pride: he always wanted to fabricate his own rig and now has. He worked on it all winter. On Saturdays and Sundays Murdoch would come over and swamp, help him out. Ed understands Murdoch. What Murdoch wants is to be a welder, but needs practice before he can go for his ticket. He works hard. He is twenty years old, two years older than Chris, Ed and Myrtle's son, whom Ed believes to be a queer.

Murdoch can't understand Lubnickie. He is tickled by the idea of ladies working with them. Two of the gals look good and Murdoch hopes one of them will be picked to work with Ed and him on their little odds-and-ends crew.

His mind envisions an on-the-road fling. Contrary to what many people believed, you didn't get much tail on the road. Due to bad publicity brought on by certain construction crews in the fifties and sixties, mothers aren't pleased when the trucks roll into town. Curtains snap shut, doors slam, and young girls are yanked inside for their own good. You get lonely and all there is to do is get drunk and shoot pool with bar derelicts.

It would be great, Murdoch thinks, to have an affair with a gal you worked with. Staying in company-paid rooms, both making good money, banking a lot. Taking a winter holiday to Acapulco or somewhere (they were both working, they could afford it). Working for a few more years to stash away some cash, getting married, having a kid or two, buying a starter home. It'd be tough—sure—things were tough these days. She'd have to quit her job and stay home (none of this day-care crap for Murdoch's kids; none of this McDonald's and Dairy Queen every night). He hoped she'd still let him play softball and hunt with the boys, but maybe she wouldn't. Money'd be tight, and why should she be expected to stay home with the kids all day

and all night while he was out having fun? But hell, a guy needed that. If she didn't like it, too bad. He made the money and
he deserved a reward.

Murdoch listens as Finch reads off the girls' names, and he's
bummed right out. The two nice babes get put on other crews
and the sour-looking one is assigned to him and Ed. Life just
ain't fair sometimes.

Myrtle Lubnickie watches through the window. Murdoch's
flatbed with the Ditch Witch chained to the trailer like a giant
praying mantis pulls in front of the house. He and a girl get out
and approach Ed. Ed throws something on the lawn, then picks
it up. Myrtle can hear his voice even from inside though she
can't quite make out what he is saying. The girl and Murdoch
get back in the flatbed and drive away. A short time later, Lubnickie backs his rig out of the drive and leaves in the same direction. Myrtle wonders who the girl is. She doesn't look much
younger than herself.

The job site is in a new subdivision in the city. Next week
they will head out on the road. They park the vehicles on the
crusted clay ground and Lubnickie lays down the rules. He's a
professional welder and that's all he does. Murdoch is an equip-
ment operator and does Lubnickie's fitting. Norma is to pull
the tubing to the house, tap the tee after Lubnickie welds it to
the main line, tie the tubing into the house, paint the riser gray,
and do any shovel work Murdoch needs help with.

"Come on, Eddy," Murdoch says. "And what are you going
to be doing while she does all that?"

"Sitting in my truck, listening to the radio. You got a problem with that?" Lubnickie snaps the cheaters open and the
Ditch Witch seems to sigh as the chains loosen. "And you can
start by doing this," he says to Norma, walking to the rear of the
flatbed. "These are called beaver tails. It'll be your job to pull
them down so Murdoch can back the Ditch Witch off."

Norma grabs one of the beaver tails. They look like cast-iron
stove racks and there is one on each corner of the flatbed. She
yanks the handle and hurts something in her arm. She bends

her legs and tries to push up on the handle. Nothing happens.

"Get serious, Ed." Murdoch grabs the handle, grunts, and slowly pulls the beaver tail so it turns on its hinge. It slams to the earth and Norma's feet jump. "These are ramps," Murdoch tells Norma. "I'll get them." He looks at Ed. "They're too heavy."

"Do her share if you want," Lubnickie says.

"We were doing everything just the two of us till this morning," Murdoch says. "With three of us it should be easier."

Lubnickie says, "We've got a utility man now, so I'm just going to do what I'm paid for."

"Look," says Norma, "I don't want to ruin anybody's life, I just want a job, OK?"

Norma comes home after her first day of work to find Tracy making french fries, dropping frozen slivers into the snapping oil. She has shaved crescents like moons above her ears and dresses more like a whore than a fourteen year old. She is smoking one of Norma's roll-your-owns. Her schoolbooks are piled on top of the fridge, the covers scrawled with name-filled hearts and sketches of syringes and marijuana leaves. If Norma wasn't so exhausted, she believes she might cuff the girl. Terry, who is twelve, but only in fourth grade due to his dyslexia, is absorbed in a pocket of silence in front of the TV.

"Where's your father?" Norma asks Tracy.

"How should I know? Can I send Terry to the store for some ketchup and vinegar?"

"With what? I don't get paid till the end of the month."

"Well, don't get mad at me."

Norma looks at Terry, the back of his head framed by the TV screen, his legs oddly askew as if he's paralyzed. "Sorry," she says truthfully.

She gets in the car, a rusted 1968 Pontiac Parisienne that is gone in the rods and tie ends and sways down the street like a boat. She parks it near the bar and sees Colin's Harley angled in front with some other motorcycles. He is inside at a table full of beer and ribs in paper trays. Two women, two men.

"Hi babe," Colin says when he sees her. He looks so good in his black leather vest and tight jeans, more like twenty-five than almost forty. He has his shirt open and his gold chain showing. "I was just talking about your new job."

"You're lucky to be working," one of the girls says. Norma recognizes her from parties, but doesn't know her name for sure. She quit this scene a long time ago, it seems. The girl is wearing a leather vest like Colin's, but without a shirt underneath. She has peroxide hair, dark sooty eyes, and expensive high-heeled boots. She asks Colin for some quarters to play some tunes and he gives her two.

"The kids want me to pick up some things at the store," Norma says, "so can I have some money?" She knows this is embarrassing to Colin, but is beyond caring.

"Sure, babe." Colin smiles at the bearded man across from him. The girl returns, wriggles back onto her chair, and Colin puts some crumpled bills on the table. They open up like they are blossoming and Colin pushes them at Norma, making a show of it.

Outside, Norma is getting in the car when Colin comes out. "Didn't they pay you today?"

"It's not that kind of job, Colin. They hold back two weeks. I don't want you down here all the time when I'm at work."

"I need that money back," Colin says.

Murdoch's apartment is in a new subdivision where single people supposedly stay. It has four large white rooms with gyprock walls, plush shag carpet, and no insulation. Wind whistles through invisible cracks in the walls and rustles the jug of dry, spray-painted weeds beside the stucco fireplace Murdoch doesn't use. In his living room he has a matching couch, love seat, and chair. There is a glass coffee table with a TV Guide on it and a bowl of soggy cereal. In his bedroom stands the biggest waterbed money can buy with piles of magazines beside it. On the shelf above the fireplace is a row of painted beer steins with tin lids, an empty whiskey bottle shaped like a Volkswagen Beetle, and an upturned vodka bottle rigged with a hose and metal rack to look like an intravenous, $M*A*S*H$ stenciled on it in red. He has records of the Oak Ridge Boys, Peter Frampton,

Willy Nelson, Rush, Bob Seger, Dolly Parton, Sting—he probably couldn't list them all.

When he gets home from work he opens a beer and turns on "Gilligan." It's a repeat.

Murdoch wonders if he should go to the Snug again, pay the cover charge, and feel out of place as usual. Last time he went he wore his white pants and expensive mauve shirt, and people stared at him like he walked in out of another era. Maybe he should just stay home and practice combing his hair.

Lubnickie's rumpus room sports a stuffed fish, two deer heads, a framed hunter safety diploma. This is where he goes to feel at home. There is a stand-up gun rack that looks like a china cabinet, a Remington pump action 30-06, a rare Winchester lever-action 30-30 with a centennial gold coin in the stock, and a lever-action single shot .22 by Ithaca. On the walls hang an antique goose gun, some neat old double-barrels, his buck knife on a protruding screw, a braided quirt and hackamore halter hanging from a prong on one of the deer heads, a stuffed pheasant. There is one chair and a small desk full of Myrtle's yarn patterns. Also there is Myrtle's deepfreeze. Everything Lubnickie ever wanted in a home is in this room. Everything he's ever wanted. Sometimes he'll come down just to smell the gun bluing and sit alone. Maybe read a Louis L'Amour, or dust the deer heads. He comes down here to remember that these are the things he dreamed of having someday, and why he worked so hard. A house, a wife who doesn't cat around, a son. Sometimes he comes down here to escape Myrtle's vacuum and Chris's stereo.

"Tracy, I don't *have* any money," Norma says again. "I'm sorry, I just don't."

"Everybody else gets to go to the show." Tracy is sighing tearfully, flapping her arms to her sides like she's trying to fly.

"I want a lot of things I can't have, too," Norma says.

Tracy swings her purse at the fridge and something smashes inside. She glares at Norma. "I can't wait to get out of here," she hisses.

Norma sighs. "I can't either, Tracy." She is tired. Tired of being phoned by the school people, tired of watching for the unlit cruiser that has slid in front of the house more than once with Tracy inside. Just tired. Weary of feeling so young when she's expected to be wise.

"Fuck you too, Mom." Tracy crying softly. She reaches in her purse for a Kleenex and brings out a piece of glass from a broken perfume bottle, cheap aroma filling the air.

Lubnickie scowls at his wife and nods his head toward his son Chris.

"Don't read at the table, Chris," Myrtle says. "You know it upsets Dad."

Chris has soft blue eyes, short, feathered hair, and fine features like a bird. He looks like Myrtle.

"Another PCB spill." He folds the paper to another page.

"What bullshit," Lubnickie says. "When I started to work in the warehouse we unloaded transformers full of that stuff all the time. It'd pour out like water when we tipped them. Hell, I've stood up to my knees in PCBs, and now everybody's panicking about a few drops on the highway."

"You worked in PCBs?" Chris says. "You never told me about that."

"And look at me. I'm fine. It's just the newspapers trying to scare idiots who believe everything they read. Like you. Now your mother told you to put that paper down."

Chris drops the paper on the floor.

"Tell me, Dad, when you worked in the PCBs, was that before or after I was born?"

Murdoch tries unsuccessfully for an hour to find a girl who will go to the Snug with him, and then *his* phone rings. He lets it ring four times, his palm hovering over the receiver, before he picks it up. But it's only a guy from work wanting to go out and quaff a few beers in a seedy bar for working men. Murdoch begs off and watches TV for a while. He has the sensation that his face is sliding off the bones and his brains are leaking out. *If this is my real life, show me a sign.* At nine o'clock, he showers, pats his pits and back with white antisweat powder, gargles, hairsprays his head to make his cut work, dumps back three quick beers for courage, and pilots his Camaro to the Snug.

There is a line-up as usual. And, as usual, people are being pulled from behind Murdoch by the bouncer. How do they do that? Murdoch comes here at least twice a week when he's working in town, and still nobody seems to know him. As he takes out his wallet for the cover-charge girl, he says, "Hi, Ellen."

Ellen looks at him, wearily.

Murdoch laughs. "I saw your name tag."

"Three fifty," Ellen says.

The Snug is the most popular nightspot in town for singles action. It is a huge Quonset affair, the kind Murdoch has seen combines parked in, and it is lit by hundreds of swirling strobe lights. Above the dance floor a great ball of prisms revolves like a world of glass. Murdoch often catches himself staring at this when he comes here, wondering about how it works. It looks quite small and manageable, but he knows it is bigger than he is.

Murdoch makes his way to a table and sits alone, admiring the snake pit action of the dance floor. Sometimes he imagines himself at the center of the floor, spinning handsomely, but not very often because he can't dance. Not that he ever tried when he wasn't too drunk to walk straight. He spots three good-looking women sitting manless and tries to imagine one sitting beside him, her leg against his.

After a few drinks, Murdoch tells the waitress to send a round to the girls' table. They are all drinking Zombies. Fourteen dollars worth. They giggle at each other when the drinks arrive, and when the waitress points out Murdoch they wave daintily and giggle some more. Murdoch smiles back and raises an index finger. They go back to talking, and it appears that they are deciding who should come over to talk to Murdoch or if they all should, or if they should invite him to their table.

Murdoch smiles at his luck and drunk courage and weaves to the bathroom. It is at the end of a narrow, dim, blue hallway. A yellow light cuts under the door. Things are looking up. Inside, four rough-looking types lean on the sinks and pass a joint around. They are trying not to laugh. When they leave, a fat guy in pants like Murdoch's comes in. He nods at Murdoch and drops his white pants to his knees in front of the full-length mirror and starts shaving the stubble on his crotch with a Bic razor. Murdoch backs out the door, keeping his eyes on the fat, naked ass speckled with heat blisters and ingrown hairs.

His table is taken when he returns. He wonders if the girls left or if they were ever there.

Of the three on the little odds-and-ends crew, Murdoch probably finds things the hardest. Lubnickie welds his tee on the main line, and that's it. Norma doesn't know what's going on, and though she tries, after a week, trying doesn't cut it anymore.

Murdoch is the one who digs the bell hole with the small claw of the Ditch Witch. Murdoch trenches the slash from the bell hole to the house with the chain saw blade on the back of the Witch. It's Murdoch who fits the regulator swing, screws it into the house, and then it's *Murdoch who helps Norma* pull the tubing pipe, tap the tee to the main, tie the tubing to the house, purge the line, paint the riser, draw the as-built, and backfill the service. Norma has seen Murdoch looking at her, swearing to himself, but she doesn't know what to do.

At coffee, nobody talks. When they drive somewhere in the same truck, they sit bone rigid on the bouncing seat and look straight ahead. It's so bad the first week that Norma can't believe it when it gets worse in week two.

They are working out of the city in a small town. Lubnickie drives from one job to the next purposely leaving Norma behind. Murdoch follows him in the flatbed without realizing.

"Where's Norma at?" he asks Lubnickie as they sit on the rim of a houseless basement, waiting.

"Maybe she quit."

"Give me your keys and I'll go look for her," says Murdoch.

"Not in my truck, you won't."

So Murdoch takes the flatbed, retracing the streets to the last job. He finds Norma wandering the sidewalk, about to cry.

That night in the same small town, Lubnickie, the foreman of the crew, doesn't book Norma a room in the hotel, knowing she is too broke to pay for one herself and too proud to ask Murdoch for money. Murdoch, in the bar watching the ball game, doesn't find out that she spent the night in the flatbed until the next day at noon.

They are working in a town so small that there is no café, so they eat jungle lunch out of cans. Lubnickie has the only opener. When Norma asks if she can borrow it after Murdoch is done, Lubnickie says, "Not likely."

"What the hell, Ed?" says Murdoch.

"It's OK," Norma says. "If I can spend a night in a truck, I'm sure I'll survive missing one meal." She heaves her can of beans into the trees and some birds fly up.

"What do you mean?" asks Murdoch. "What does she mean, Ed?"

"Don't ask me what the bitch is talking about," Lubnickie laughs.

And Murdoch is up, pushing his hands against Lubnickie's chest. It feels weird: this is his hero.

"Settle down, stud," Lubnickie warns. "I've been around a long time. I'll get you both run off."

Friday night, Norma returns home to her children who are eating Alpha Bits for supper. She feels like she's home from the wars and could use some hugs, but the kids act like she's only been in another room for a few hours. She drifts into the living room and discovers a saucepan of Kraft Dinner on the TV with a spoon stuck in it. When Norma lifts the spoon, the whole saucepan comes up. Ashtrays, Coke and beer bottles are everywhere on the stained carpet, arranged almost artistically. Norma bends, gathers empty Hostess bags and licorice wrappers off the floor. Shards of potato chips embedded in the carpet swarm like a galaxy in Norma's blurred eyes.

"Where's your Dad?"

"How am I supposed to know?" says Tracy.

And Norma is upon her. She clutches Tracy's hair with one hand and moves the other back and forth across her daughter's face. Tracy twisting away. The table making a grating sound, bouncing on its flimsy aluminum legs across the linoleum. Bowls sliding off, making white bursts on the floor. There is screaming, a door opening. Tracy holds a bread knife in front of her. So much screaming. Where is Terry? Norma turns, sees him in the corner, holding himself in a way she never could.

Midnight, Colin's Harley roars up the street and sputters into silence. He enters a spotless house smelling of Mister Clean and Pine Sol. Norma sees him from the chesterfield in front of the TV. He walks across the shiny floor in his black boots with the buckles. Norma feels his nearness on her. She is in her housecoat and slippers, the pink nighty she sometimes wears underneath.

"How was your week?" Colin asks.

"Colin, it was—"

"Listen, babe, could I have a twenty for a couple of hours?" He looks at her. "Just a couple of hours."

Norma gets the purse with the one missing strap, fishes for the money. The world is whirling and making a buzzing noise in her head. She hands over the money.

"You don't know how hard it is for a man like me to have to beg like this," Colin says. Rolls the bill like a joint, buries it in the pocket of his vest.

"When will you be back?"

"I got some things to do."

"What things? Tracy's gone."

Colin glances around the room. "Look, I'll be back when I get back."

The Harley disappears like closing a zipper. Norma goes into the bedroom and puts some clothes in a suitcase, then takes them out. She pulls Colin's shirts from the closet, lays them on the bed, looks at them. She goes to the kid's room and Terry is asleep. Tracy's bed is unmade but empty.

It is well after midnight. Norma pulls on the TV and watches an old movie without interest. She cannot follow the plot, can't figure out what's going on. Finally, she sleeps while the TV snows. If Norma dreams, she never remembers.

When Lubnickie gets home, Myrtle has already gone to Royal Purple. He is surprised that he doesn't mind. He just doesn't. Chris is there, wearing short pants and running shoes, fooling around with his basketball. Eighteen years old, still asking for allowance. It is something for Lubnickie to marvel at. When he was Chris's age, Chris was already born.

"Put some coffee on for the old man, would you, son?"

"Sure." And Chris as usual does the Chris thing. He pours coffee grounds into the tea kettle, burns out the element.

"How in hell can you live to be eighteen and not know how to make coffee?" Lubnickie cries, kitchen full of smoke.

"I just never took an interest in it, I guess."

"But you got to."

"Why?"

"Because I gave you a job to do."

"So?"

"So you're a man, son. Someday you're going to have to support a family with your work."

"Why?"

"Because that's the way it is."

"But what if I don't have a job I like?"

"Wake up. Nobody likes their job except the bums on welfare."

"Then why don't they quit?"

"Because they have a family to support!"

"Calm down, Dad."

Lubnickie descends the stairs to his rumpus room. He dusts the plastic muzzles of the deer heads, takes down his quirt, draws it through the air. He unsheathes his knife, checks its edge with his thumb, and gets out the oilstone.

Maybe I come down here for the old days, but those days were pretty damn good in my books, he thinks. Men were men. Lubnickie met Myrtle at a dance. She was flowing across the dance floor, and he said to a buddy from work that he was going after that one no matter who she came with. And he did. And it never got any better than that moment.

Lubnickie is sitting in the dark room, listening to the faint thump of his son's stereo upstairs. Deer skulls stare over him. He is populated by fulfilled dreams, emptied by them.

On Saturday morning, Murdoch goes fishing with a girl he met the night before at the Snug. They drive to a nearby lake, stand knee-deep in yellow bromegrass and cast out. He watches the girl. She knows what she is doing. Her moves are delicate, skilled. Murdoch's own rod whips the air friskily.

But after an hour all they've caught is a carp with a tumor on its belly. They throw it back and eat sandwiches on a spread-out blanket. They drink beer while grasshoppers arc over them like burned-out fireworks.

Sun going down pinkly, wind chamois soft; it's too much for Murdoch, who rolls the girl off the blanket into the spear grass. She rolls over him and they are rolling. Murdoch feels like he's in an Elvis beach movie. He nearly starts crooning at the girl.

On the way back to Murdoch's Camaro, they start to talk about mutual acquaintances. She knows every guy Murdoch knows. Intimately, it turns out. Murdoch is holding his boots in his hands, concentrating on the sharp parts of the ground, and when he hears this it throws off his balance and causes him to step off the path and drive a cactus spike deep in his heel. It is sunk so deep the girl has to pry it out with the needle-nose pliers Murdoch keeps in his tackle box. Murdoch nearly passes out from the pain of it all.

Infection sets in. Monday morning everybody will ask him what he caught on the weekend, but he won't know for a couple of days.

Lubnickie leans up the ramp. "What in hell happened to your wheel, stud?"

Murdoch has an oversized running shoe on his infected foot. He could have taken the day off with pay, even the week, but what would he do if he wasn't working?

"Don't worry about it. I'll be able to get around."

"A cripple and a woman and yourself. Sounds like a real production outfit, Eddy," one of the other foremen says. "How's your honey panning out anyways?"

"Don't remind me," Lubnickie says. "How about yours?"

"She fucked off. They all did except yours. You must be treating her special, are you?"

"Yeah, he is," says Murdoch.

Lubnickie checks his wristwatch. "She's late this morning.

Maybe she packed it in, too." He claps Murdoch on the back. "Could be just me and Long John Silver this week."

The Parisienne dies at an intersection about half a mile from the shop, so Norma gets to work fifteen minutes late, on foot. Lubnickie is laying on his rig seat, boots out the window, paring his fingernails with his jackknife.

"It's about time. *Murdoch,* let's go!"

Murdoch limps over. "He took a girl out and she shot him in the foot on the weekend," Lubnickie says.

"Where's your car?" Murdoch asks Norma.

Nobody is more surprised than Norma when she starts to cry. Tracy's gone. Colin didn't come home. She had to find a babysitter for Terry for the week. She thought she'd be fired for being late. She tries not to, but she says some of this along with what the car was doing when it quit.

"Doesn't sound too serious," Lubnickie says. "Sounds like it's only a loose connection or something minor."

"Sorry," Norma says.

"Well, let's get it running so we can get on the road," Lubnickie says to Murdoch.

"It's too much trouble," Norma insists.

"You're not leaving your car on the side of the road all goddamn week." Lubnickie starts up his rig, and Norma slides in beside him.

Thursday night. They are staying in a small town with a nightclub, so Lubnickie and Murdoch go to check out the live music. Lubnickie can't believe it. Mike, Mark, Jack—the Rhythm Pals. Older, slack-bodied, and toupeed, but wearing the same Roy Rogers outfits, singing the same mournful harmonies they sang in Lubnickie's youth on radio and TV.

He orders drink after drink, watches the dancers, most of them kids moving like mimes trying to cross a forcefield. In his day Lubnickie and Myrtle—well. . . . His cowboy heel clicks the floor.

Murdoch erects his infected foot on the arm of a chair. He can't believe it either. Who are these old dudes and why isn't anybody throwing things at them? He is matching Lubnickie drink for drink in an attempt to kill the pain and pretend he's at the Snug. Also to forget that his real life begins . . . when?

Norma phones home, gets nothing. Lubnickie gave her some expense money and it is arranged on the hotel bed. All but the eight dollars she spent on a mickey of rum. She takes a small drink out of the plastic hotel glass and looks out the window. She hears the music blowing across the street and knows the sound from her parent's record collection. When she was a teenager she used to watch the Rhythm Pals on "The Tommy Hunter Show."

Norma knows Lubnickie will be in the lounge when she gets there, and a decision will have to be made. Sit by yourself and get hit on, or with a man who hates your guts.

Murdoch is yawning, watching the door. He motions Norma over. She has done something with her hair—put it up, and has on a pair of large hoop earrings she took from Tracy's box. She looks fun. Has perfume on.

"It's called makeup," she says to Murdoch. "Don't stare too hard." Lubnickie still hasn't looked at her. "I used to listen to them on the radio," she half-yells giddily.

Lubnickie looks at her now, and Murdoch says, "You're kidding." He tries to imagine her seated with her grandparents around an old wooden radio with cloth on the front and a dome top.

Norma orders a Paralyzer, knowing it will be a rip-off, but she feels like it tonight. No Colin, no nothing. This week she drove the Ditch Witch off the flatbed and it was no different from backing up a standard. She trenched out a service. She did some things she didn't believe she was capable of. And she wasn't the only one.

"Dance?" she yells over the music, tapping Murdoch on the back.

He points at his raised foot. "I can't," he admits, "ask Ed."

No way.

Murdoch nudges Lubnickie in the side with his bad foot. When Lubnickie turns, Murdoch motions with his head to Norma.

What can he do? Lubnickie thinks. She is smiling at him.

They move woodenly to the floor and hold onto each other arthritically. Lubnickie is sweating, clumping his feet. He's a good dancer, usually, but his timing's off tonight. Norma hums along, tries to turn him every once in a while. The song ends and Norma hooks an arm around Lubnickie for a second to keep him up there.

"I'm drunk." She smiles at him.

"I'm out of practice," he says. "It's hard to keep my feet under me."

"Thanks for fixing my car. You're a good dancer if you want to know."

The next song is old and takes Lubnickie back. He loosens, flows with the tempo. Halfway through the dance, he takes the hand Norma rests on his back and tucks it in his own back pocket, and they move around like that. The way he used to. The song changes to something new and Norma steers Lubnickie through the throngs of young dancers, aware he thinks he is doing the leading.

Murdoch, watching from the table, smiles at a certain waitress each time she passes. Finally she tells him to get lost. Murdoch nods his head in acceptance, but wonders how much more lost she means? He watches Norma and Lubnickie dance—the way they move together and apart, trying to keep their balance with all the changing shapes around them.

$\mathcal{T}$HE EYE

$\mathcal{H}$arvey McKinnon was hopelessly eye-shy, whatever the situation. In lines he trembled for fear some lunatic might stick his face up into his own demanding a match or the time of day. On walks along the beach, he sadly averted his eyes from the son he saw only on alternate weekends. In bars, he ricocheted conversations off ashtrays and beer mugs rather than meeting the eyes of his girlfriend Mavis. In his cab he put masking tape over the rearview mirror and refused to talk to passengers as he took them to their destinations. If Harvey McKinnon was nuttier than a fruitcake, as he liked to put it himself, he knew the blame had to be shared by the eyes of a butchered pig.

Harvey wheeled the battered Plymouth that served as his cab into the parking lot of Stan's All Nite Diner, and radioed that he was booking off for breakfast. It looked like rain. Dark clouds swept in over the harbor promising a rush hour of wet and bitter paying customers. He took a six-person booth with a window view and waited for Mavis.

She burst through the swinging kitchen doors in a brown and orange flutter of Fortrel. "More coffee, folks?" she asked a couple of tired lovers who were sharing the same small space. Harvey marveled as she bent to pour the coffee. So carefully. As if she was pouring herself and didn't want to spill.

"Big Guy Breakfast?" she asked Harvey as she whisked past.

"Two eggs, easy over, and ham," he replied, "with hash browns, coffee, and whole wheat toast." He gave her the cool smile she liked as she vanished into the kitchen with a tray of dirty cups.

When she came back with his coffee, Harvey was staring

numbly out the window. A gaunt man with a nicked face and sunglasses stared back. Harvey no longer had mirrors at home and shaved by feel.

"Something the matter, honey?" Mavis asked him.

Harvey shook his head. "Listen, something happened this afternoon." He glanced around, whispering, "You got a minute?"

"Can it wait till I'm off shift?"

It was 5:30 A.M. Mavis would be done in an hour. Harvey shrugged. It was starting to rain, and he had only done twenty clear tonight including no tips, but he guessed it could wait. He had nothing but time. "I'll be here, my sweet," he said.

When Mavis was gone, Harvey jerked a napkin out of the metal dispenser and uncapped his pen. How does this one fit in? he wondered. He pounded his chest and let out a silent burp. First pigs, now potatoes. The pain in his guts was killing him.

He spread the napkin open on the table. Maybe Mavis would be able to understand it. In any case, Harvey sensed the end; it had come to this, and now he had to finish it. Licking the tip of his pen, he hunched over and wrote: *The Potato Eye* . . .

Eyes were the curse of Harvey McKinnon. Eighteen months ago he was a schoolteacher in a place called Saskatchewan. He lived with a quiet wife and a four-year-old son, David. He was, you know, happy. Then one rainy Sunday in September he went to a fellow teacher's farm to help butcher a pig, and his life was altered.

The split second before the .22 smacked a red, dime-sized hole into the pig's forehead just above the snout, one of the pig's small dark eyes met Harvey's own. The pig was howling and pawing manure, but the eye was very calm and certain. In a voice that crackled in his ears like a long-distance telephone call, a voice that apparently only Harvey could hear, it said: "The jester should never kill the king. Au revoir."

Harvey smiled self-consciously and looked over at Bill whose farm it was, but Bill wasn't paying attention. Then, as suddenly as it had spoken, the pig was dead. Harvey squatted and looked into the unsparkling sad eyes and felt a mysterious stirring inside him, a strange uneasiness.

Later, when the pig was butchered and divided into the

trunks of cars, Harvey walked back out to the manure pile and watched the chickens pecking the eyes out of the pig's severed head and the tension within him subsided. But then Shirley, Harvey's wife, yelled from the yard, "What's eating you? Do you want to take half-a-dozen broilers home, too?"

The feeling recommenced, thrumming through him. It was getting worse.

That night came the first dream: A man wearing a trench coat is pursued down a blind alley. At the wall, nowhere to turn, he reaches his fingers into his eye socket, tears the eye out, and hides it in his breast pocket. "They'll never find me here," he says. And indeed they don't; the pursuers and the pursued exit the alley together, the hidden eye the only disguise.

The dream recurred quite often, but Harvey only remembered vague fragments. It wasn't until early October when he had the second dream that he became concerned. This dream was so vivid that it left him with the odd waking sensation of standing in the mouth of a blind alley, footsteps retreating on the gleaming concrete.

During recess in the staff room, he wrote:

Eye Spy Dream #2

Trenchcoat man is pursued
to rail of iron bridge
Water below is dark
He looks around
reaches into face
tears out eye—
egg in moonlight
wet and mucus
small boiled pierogi—
(you'll never find me here
he cries)
and heaves the spinning orb
far out into water
dark as a throat

"Is that what they call modern poetry?" Bill was absently reading over Harvey's shoulder.

Harvey looked at the paper, startled at what he'd written. Fortunately he didn't have to dream up an excuse because Bill had already lost interest. He was punching the buttons of a computer game, probably confiscated from a broken-hearted student.

This dream, like Eye Spy Dream #1, was recurring, and though not really frightening, its persistence took a toll. Harvey wanted to talk about it; to get it off his chest, but what could he say? I have been spoken to by the eye of a pig? Who would believe it—Bill? No, Bill was a good guy, but he taught math with an iron fist. He was only thirty-two and his favorite "rock" group was the Canadian Brass. The most he could do would be to confirm what Harvey already suspected: that he was cracking up.

That Sunday Harvey was on the hammock, busy absorbing an unusually warm October sun in his fenced-in backyard. He was just nicely started into a six-pack of beer, just nicely getting into the spirit of the football game on the radio when he heard: "Bonjour. You have accomplished less in your life than I did in mine. Welcome aboard." Harvey spun the dial on the radio so hard it slipped off its runner. But the voice wasn't coming from the radio. "Bonjour," it said, "au revoir."

Harvey looked up toward heaven and saw a small cloud cover the sun that burned from behind it like the dark eye of a pig.

Sweet Jesus, he thought, I'm cracking up.

"Daddy!" David came skipping down the back steps. "Mommy says to light the barbecue now."

Something tried to kick its way out of Harvey's stomach. He thrashed and swung for balance, but pitched off the hammock onto the lawn. "Hi," said his son's eyes, "that loser is my dad!"

He was in a heap on the grass, face buried in his hands, when Shirley came out and stood on the back step. "Harvey, what in the world—"

He looked up at the chubby, crop-headed matron who had somehow become his wife. And when he looked into her eyes that, though silent, seemed to be saying, "My husband is a wimp and I'm a loser in my own right," he started to cry. The sun peeked out from behind the cloud, and he sprinted past his wife and child into the house where he took a spatula to every mirror, every single pane of glass.

He tried to teach for a while after this, but dreaded facing the hundreds of student eyes that burned him with insults hour after hour. He resigned at the end of October, leaving a very unhappy Bill to teach his eighth-grade English class in his only prep period until a suitable replacement could be found.

"Harve," Bill joked at the going-away party, "how can you do this to me after all I've done for you?"

Ironic. For in a way Harvey held Bill partly responsible for what was being labeled a nervous breakdown: It *had* been Bill's farm. He looked Bill in the receding hairline (he'd figured out by now that eye contact aggravated the tension), and said, "I've been spoken to by the pig who is largely responsible for the sandwich you're eating."

Friends recommended he check himself into the psych ward, but Harvey refused. Part of his problem, he was convinced, was these very people and the things they stood for. Thanks to their guidance and feedback he had flourished into the nut case he now knew himself to be. He had retirement funds in the bank, but only one oar in the water. He had to get away, to escape.

Also there was the ever-watchful prairie sun. Harvey felt its steady arc of time was partly to blame for leading him prematurely into his dotage. So he sold the bungalow, loaded Shirley and David into the Plymouth, and struck out for the coast, where it rained more than shined.

For one instant, as they loaded the car, Harvey had doubts. He wanted Shirley to reach out and hold him, choke him even; to demand something of him. "Who *are* you, you fraud?" he wanted her to say. "What have you done with my husband?" But instead she just sat in the back seat, as far away from Harvey as she could get, and covered her face with a magazine.

The trip was not a pleasant one.

Shirley wanted to know what the hell Harvey thought he was doing? Was he expecting welfare to support them in the lifestyle they were accustomed to? What kind of a man was he? And the sun gnawed at the emptiness that clung to Harvey's ribs. In the mountains he solved at least part of the problem by purchasing mirrored sunglasses (aviator style) for himself, horn-rims for Shirley (which she liked but refused to wear), and little red plastic ones for David.

Once settled on the coast, Shirley found work as a receptionist with an accounting firm, and met Alan, a chartered accountant who wanted to marry her. Harvey wasn't surprised. Shirley had worried off quite a few pounds and was getting handsome.

"I'm moving in with a man I work with," she informed Harvey one evening. "I can't live like this anymore."

Harvey was silent. Rain angled into the windows, the plush sod outside.

"I need more—"

Harvey said he understood, staring out the window at the welcome rain.

Shirley started to cry very softly. "Why?" She asked him. Over the past months her questions had converged to a single *why?* Harvey sighed and started to explain, but before he could, Shirley ran over and slapped the glasses off his nose. "And don't tell me about a goddamn pig's eye! You copped out, admit it! You can't take it!"

"Take what?"

"Responsibility!"

"You're nuts." Harvey picked up his shades, put them back on.

"Yeah, it's me." Shirley was crying hard now, really feeling it. "I'm the crazy one all right."

She took everything but the car. When she was gone, Harvey sat in the emptiness of the apartment and felt the void inside him diminish a little.

That wonderfully wet and dark winter Harvey got a job driving a cab, and moved into a co-op house with some artsy students where he fast became a cult figure: the older guy who gave up teaching to drive hack. How bohemian.

It was also during this winter that he met Mavis Sears.

On a frigid, rainy morning, Harvey was hoping to pick up a few pedestrians willing to stave off pneumonia by coughing up a taxi fare when he spotted her. A deer wrapped in a raincoat, hurdling the fresh pools of rain, her legs hammering out from under her orange skirt. Harvey screeched the Plymouth to a halt and, with chivalrous flare, leaped out and swung open the passenger door. "Can I offer you a lift?"

Mavis let out a thin scream. A puff of frozen breath appeared. As she backed away, shaking her head, Harvey cursed himself for having to wear sunglasses even in the dark.

"Go away!" she pleaded.

But Harvey was already gathering speed to clear the puddle that separated Mavis from him. She wasn't the only athletic one.

He landed stiff-kneed on the slick cement, his legs skiing up with such force that he was horizontal with the earth, a human luge aimed at her heart. His feet thumped into Mavis, propelling her backwards into a hedge. His own head came to rest on the street. He didn't feel the icy water washing over him or see his sunglasses go down the storm grate.

For reasons, Harvey later learned, closer to adventure than pity, Mavis slumped him into the cab and drove him to her suite where she doctored the egg on the back of his skull and warmed him with steamy chicken soup and a hot bath. Then for reasons, Mavis was quick to point out, closer to curiosity than lust, she warmed him in her bed.

Bruised, in love, scraped, Harvey lay listening to Mavis's breathing rustle the sheets. Was he just a pin marking one morning on a map of sexual exploration? Was he? "Mavis," he said, "be honest, are you glad I ran into you, or what?" He was only half-joking.

"Did Prince Charming come in a Plymouth?" she asked.

"It takes a big pig to weigh a ton," he admitted.

Mavis rolled into his arms, breath skittering like mosquito feet across his eyelashes.

"Please don't ever look into my eyes," Harvey said. He was clutching her warmth. Outside, rain clattered onto the sidewalk.

"You're a strange one," Mavis said. "Anybody ever tell you that before?"

For what seemed like an eternity Harvey tried to be strong and silent, but the role no longer fit, if it ever had. "Eyes talk to me," he blurted, "pig eyes, headlights, light bulbs, the moon . . ." He watched her lips for movement. They parted and lifted at the corners, and he saw a tiny silver filling on a back molar. "Don't laugh," he said, but he wished he hadn't said anything at all.

"Do my eyes . . . you know?"

Harvey couldn't say. He hadn't looked into them and knew he never would.

That night he dreamed they were birds. He had gone blind and Mavis was leading him back to Saskatchewan though she had no idea where the place was. As they flew, his beak holding her tail, eastward from the sea, Mavis described the world below.

"Tall mountains," she said.

"Not Saskatchewan," he replied.

"Huge cities down there."

"Nope."

"How about something shaped like a coffin for somebody in a large hat—"

"Take us down, Mavis."

A strong draft caught Harvey, tearing him away from Mavis's tail, and flung him downward, end over end like a badly thrown football. He crashed headfirst into an uprooted tree. The blow miraculously restored his sight and he saw Mavis, multicolored and bright, circling against the sky. Then he saw he was surrounded by thousands of sad gray sparrows pecking at scattered grain in the snow. His own feathers were turning gray and he flapped his wings madly trying to get airborne, but the roots of the tree scratched at his eyes and snared him. He screeched for Mavis to help sever the roots with her beak. But she didn't.

Harvey awoke to the bright ring of Mavis's singing voice backed up by the hum of forced water on the walls of the shower cubicle. He quickly got dressed and made for the door. She hadn't tried to save him from the tree.

Mavis, clutching a towel to herself, intercepted him in the hallway. Harvey looked guiltily at his feet.

"So, how's your head today?" she asked, embarrassed.

"The same," Harvey nodded morosely. And then, "Oh, you mean the bump!" This brought a small laugh from Mavis. He looked at her: the slight chin, the quavering pink lips, the soft girl's moustache . . . but that was as high as he could go. He decided to level with her. "It's just that I have these dreams, you know?" Mavis allowed she had them herself. "Well, last night I dreamed I was in trouble, and you didn't try to save me. From a tree."

Mavis let out an angry whoop and stormed into the bedroom, slamming the door behind her. Harvey delicately let himself in and watched her, naked, huffing through the slanting morning light, tossing blankets around on the bed.

"Maybe I didn't save you in your dream," she said angrily, "but I saved you yesterday. *From drowning!* Besides," she added reflectively, "in dreams trees mean the past. Nobody can save you from yourself."

"Hey, come on—" but it was curious she'd say that.

"Anyhow," Mavis sulked, "I find it hard to believe I wouldn't at least try to save you. I'm a waitress, for godsakes, I serve people."

Mavis Sears was a good egg. And she learned to humor Harvey McKinnon.

"Why does this dream haunt me?" Harvey cried one morning after Eye Spy Dream #2 had spun through his sleep like a film loop. "What does it mean?"

"Well," Mavis said, crunching her toast, "you are obviously a spy."

"A spy. How do you figure that?"

"You're the guy at the airport selling contraband. The flasher. You have something under your trenchcoat you want to show the world."

"No way." Harvey shook his head, but Mavis continued. She was on a roll.

"The bridge means that you have to cross an obstacle to get something you want. An enemy is trying to stop you—" she paused for a sip of orange juice "—an enemy from your past most likely."

Shirley? Bill? Myself? Harvey wondered.

"The eye, of course, represents your view of life, your philosophy, stuff like that." Harvey was impressed. She'd obviously been giving this some thought. "And you throw your eye into the water, meaning—I don't know—you see things murky." She turned her palms upward in an all-encompassing gesture. "C'est tout."

"OK, suppose you're on the right track," Harvey challenged. "Why, pray tell, did a pig's eye speak to me in the first place?"

"Does the word *ham* mean anything to you?"

Harvey laughed self-consciously. He did have a secret desire to play his guitar on the street.

And that afternoon, for the first time, he did it. He opened his guitar case, laid open a songbook on the sidewalk beside it, and sat, his guitar balanced across his knees. All of this before the clouds broke.

As Harvey scrambled to disentangle his legs, at the same time trying to shelter his guitar from the rain, a crumpled dollar bill dropped over his shoulder into the guitar case. Through his rain-spotted glasses, Harvey looked up into the dome of his ex-wife's umbrella.

"I don't deserve this, Shirley," he said.

"Oh, I don't know, I'd say you deserve exactly that." Harvey noticed that the stubby fingers which used to knead his back during lovemaking now sported delicate silver rings. There was even a smile on her face, lipstick.

"You're looking good, Shirl," he had to admit.

"Really? You look like death warmed over." Shirley reached across and pushed Harvey's wet hair out of his eyes. She held her umbrella over them both. "David tells me you're still a good daddy though you're obviously no Alan."

Harvey had to laugh. The old, spunky Shirley, the one he originally married, had returned. He was taking partial credit for jarring her back. "Can I buy you a cup of coffee?" he asked.

"By the sounds of business, I doubt it." Shirley laughed, a guttural sexy sound that made his duodenum jump.

Coffee at Smuggler's led to a cheap room at the Sky Way Inn. Harvey watched with interest as Shirley undressed, but the interest faded when she started doing sit-ups in front of the TV before climbing onto the creaky bed.

"Well?" She bounced a breast with one hand and slammed her other fist into her stomach. "What do you think? Have I come a long way or what?"

Harvey sighed, reached to turn off the pole lamp.

"*No!* Leave it on! Alan says light is like a cup of sunshine on my skin."

Christ, Harvey thought.

He was thinking of cups with a fingerful of cold coffee, of the packed ashtrays Mavis would soon be emptying at Stan's All Nite.

"Harvey, what's eating you?" Shirley had opened her legs like an envelope. There, in the space between them, blinked an eye.

He didn't take time to answer, just scooped his clothes into his arms and ran naked into the gray drizzle of the afternoon.

A police cruiser blinked red through the rain, spun a U-turn and nosed up to the window through which Harvey was watching the coming of morning. Two policemen lumbered out. The worst, as far as eyes were concerned, had arrived. They didn't wait to be seated as the large red sign beneath the cash register instructed.

"Coffee," one of them grunted at Mavis as they settled their bulk into the booth across from Harvey and looked over at him.

Harvey imagined the torpid mental gymnastics going on behind their eyes: Is this guy wanted? An escapee maybe? Leatherette jacket, Elvis sideburns, mirrored sunglasses (at night?). What was he hiding?

Harvey waited for it to happen.

"That cab out there yours?" one of the cops would ask him. Rusted and staved-in, Harvey would have to admit the Plymouth belonged to him. It was almost all he had left to his name. "I'm an independent owner."

"That right? Well, Mister Independent, how about opening the trunk up?" the cop would whisper, knowing most cabbies carry a snort or two to occupy slack time. In fact Harvey had a partial bottle of cherry whiskey under the spare tire. "Why the shades?" The other cop would be trying to get a peek at the junkie's no doubt bloodshot eyes. "It's dark out, hey? Why don't you take them off?"

At that Harvey would snap. He'd tell them about the pig eye. They would take it wrong, bust him for some trumped-up charge, and work him over on the way to the station, careful to bruise only bones, not flesh.

But none of this happened. The cops didn't seem to care about Harvey.

"There you go, officers." Mavis set down two thick cups.

"And for you, sir," she said to Harvey, "The Big Guy Breakfast." She placed the platter on the table and sat down across from him, lighting a cigarette. "What's that you're writing, hon?" She tapped the napkin and directed a jet of smoke above his head.

Harvey had the pen clenched crosswise in his teeth. Wearily, he took it out and capped it. "I had another dream this afternoon—"

"Same old thing, huh?"

"No." Harvey put his elbows on the table and leaned across. "This dream was different, but the same, you know?" Mavis's chin bobbed up and down. "I was watching a game show on TV, right? And this commercial comes on. You know, the kind that has a kitchen appliance that dices and slices and everything else?" Mavis nodded again. She was with him. "Well, I must have dozed off, because the next thing I know there's a naked man on a mountain of julienne fries, feeding potatoes into a gigantic vegetable chopper . . . that's right, Mavis, it's real funny. Just forget it. Forget I said anything—"

She stared stonily at him and stubbed out her cigarette. "Go on."

"OK. Well, a potato gets lodged in the blades and jams the machine, so the man—I didn't see his face—he has to climb in to unplug it. To make a long story short, it starts up when he's inside, and he gets julienned. Blood and chips of bone—"

"I'm not laughing, I'm coughing!"

"The thing is, Mavis, somehow an eye survives intact, and I had the feeling—"

"Yes?"

"—I had the feeling that if I just could have reached into that dream and grabbed that eye, I'd be cured of whatever it is that's ailing me."

Mavis smiled. "That would be nice. What brought this on, I wonder?"

"I don't know," Harvey lied, thinking of Shirley, "but ever since the dream I've had a pain inside that's driving me berserk."

Mavis touched his hand. "That's because you're hungry. I've got to go and clean up. Eat your breakfast and we'll go."

She got up to leave, but Harvey caught her wrist, pulled her back down.

"This is the third eye dream."

"I know."

"Things happen in threes."

Mavis pushed the platter in front of Harvey and stood up. "I'll be ready in a few minutes. Bon appetit."

The Big Guy Breakfast was a splendid meal. White and piercing yellow eggs. Sizzling red ham that sent up an aromatic plume of lard that sparkled the air. A sprig of green parsley; four golden wedges of buttered toast. And under it all, laced with startling green onions, a neatly packed brick of hash browns.

The hollowness that had been rising in Harvey's stomach like a spiked balloon ever since he left Shirley at the motel was about to explode.

He raised his fork, gripped his knife, and saw a slice of ham move. "Bonjour."

Harvey smiled and looked over at the cops who were looking back. Had they heard? It didn't matter if they had. He felt warm half-moons of sweat spreading under his arms.

Carefully, sliding the blade of the knife under the ham, Harvey flipped it in a greasy arc onto the floor. Blinking in the center of the hash browns, there it was: a fist-sized eye, possibly a pig's.

"What are you going to do?" it taunted. "Eat me?"

As a matter of fact, Harvey didn't know what he was supposed to do, but that had never stopped him before. Eating it wasn't a bad idea, though. He picked up his fork and felt sick.

The eyeball slid back and forth across the hash browns, following the fork as Harvey passed it hand to hand, like a knife fighter. Occasionally it darted vertically or winked in defense.

"You wouldn't dare," it said, but it looked worried, and Harvey thought he detected a labored tone.

He had to.

Using the fork as a decoy, he splattered a dollop of ketchup onto the hash browns, effectively blinding the eye.

A shrill cry of pain rang out.

"Yes!" Harvey speared the eye with his fork and rammed it

between his teeth where it wriggled and squirmed like an oyster. He sucked it down without chewing, hoping to scald it with coffee. He drained his cup, scarcely feeling it.

"Mavis! A refill!"

"Here, take mine." Somebody slid a cup in front of him.

"Thanks," Harvey said, and several people said it was OK. He looked up. A crowd was gathering. But there was no time to explain.

The eggs were also eyes.

Slashing at the yolks with roundhouse curves of the fork, Harvey splattered a yellow blur into the window. He scraped it off and chewed it down, chasing it with coffee hot enough to blister the roof of his mouth.

"He's with me," he heard Mavis explaining to the officers. Harvey was beginning to panic. He had to find the ham before it found him. *"Where is it?"* he demanded.

The people in the crowd looked at each other, shrugging. Then somebody dropped the lint-covered piece of ham onto Harvey's ravaged plate. "You sure must be hungry, buddy."

Harvey slapped the ham between two slices of toast and mulched it. He splashed the remaining coffee onto his plate and lapped it up, sucking down the stem of parsley and toast crumbs. He tore a napkin from the dispenser and swabbed the plate clean. Then, leaning back, he let out a noise that sounded like it had been held captive in a bubble for a year and a half; something between a victory cry and a moan.

There was a smattering of applause. Somebody put two fingers in his mouth and whistled.

Harvey took off his shades and rubbed his eyes. They stung with sweat; he was sweating all over.

"Are you all right?" Mavis asked. Her small, warm hand felt like a bird on his own.

Harvey looked at her and smiled. Her eyes were large, like globes, and they shimmered with light. Outside, the rain had stopped and the man staring back was soaking in the morning sun, and his eyes were sky blue.

SUMMER TRAGEDY REPORT

The summer I was farmed off to my uncles' place in the country, I was thirteen, but a small thirteen. I had never set foot on a farm before, but looked forward to the adventure with the naked aplomb of youth marching into battle. I was going to live in the country and I couldn't wait for summer to start.

"And your cousin Roy from Alberta will be there too, don't forget," said my mother straightening my collar as we drove south. "You've never met him before—what do you think that will be like?"

Wonderful, was what I thought. For some reason I didn't have many friends, at least not many close friends, but somehow I knew that even though Roy was two years my senior, we would hit it off like brothers. A farm and a friend; it was really too much.

It rained the whole way there. Solid gray clouds hurtled along the tops of the telephone poles and heavy droplets splattered against the windshield of our Chevrolet. All we could pick up on the radio was the summer casualty report: a girl berry picking in the mountains had been mauled by a bear. Condition serious but stable. On the West Coast, a family singing camp songs had been attacked by a bat thought to be rabid. Closer to home, a boy of thirteen was crushed when the tractor he'd been driving overturned in the ditch. Thirteen. My mother clasped my hand.

Gradually the landscape changed from bedrock and straggly stands of timber to gently rolling farmland. Towns we passed diminished to the point where there was just a Gulf or Esso on the highway, a few maroon grain elevators strung along the tracks, and a handful of stooped houses clustered near a center street. The yard lights of farms shone like stars.

My father indicated a bluish metallic light dimmer than the rest. "That's your mother's old farm, son. What do you think?"

Before I could answer we turned off the road down a rutted drive slick with mud. At the end of the drive stood a kind of house—a slate gray structure with a roof that seemed to dip under the weight of the churning clouds. I doubted that people would actually live in there, but when we stopped the car, sure enough, Aunt Ruby was on the steps, waving us inside. She was wearing a pair of Uncle Cecil's shit-encrusted toe rubbers and had an old parka slung over her shoulders against the rain.

"There's my nephew!" she cried when I got out of the car. "Come here and let Auntie give her favorite nephew a kiss!"

My mother nudged me forward and Aunt Ruby gave me a big kiss, hoisting me off the steps when she crushed my body into hers. Something near my breastbone snapped, and I tapped experimentally at it while she called Uncle Cecil to give my parents a hand with the luggage.

"You're going to like it out here, Alex," she promised me, winking at my mother. "We're going to make a man out of you this summer."

"Swell," I said, gingerly stepping onto the porch over some rubber boots piled on a piece of newspaper.

Seeing the kitchen was a deflating experience. The floor was covered with worn linoleum torn and cracked from age and scuffing work boots. Wherever it cracked through, it curled up and was nailed back down with a neat row of upholsterer's tacks. Above the old wooden table where Uncle Chick sat, a single light bulb of inferior wattage burned dully. Bolted to the counter over the sink was a horse-snouted water pump that smelled like a mowed lawn. There was no running water, and when I asked my aunt for a drink, more or less out of curiosity, she filled a dipper from an enamel bucket. Drinking water, she said, had to be hauled from a well out back. *Hauled.*

"Chick," said Aunt Ruby to her brother-in-law, the thirty-five-year-old "baby" of the family, "Alex's been growing like a bad weed, ain't he?"

"Oh, yeah," muttered Uncle Chick. But obviously he couldn't have cared less. At least he didn't look up from his card hand. He fanned the cards out on the table and, counting to himself, marched a burnt matchstick up a cribbage board. Then he took a pull from a tumbler of whiskey.

Uncle Chick was an odd-looking duck. Unlike his brother Cecil who was red-faced and lard-assed (Dad said from drinking too much beer), or my mother, whom I considered quite attractive, Chick, as his nickname implied, had a curving beak of a nose and narrow, swarthy eyes. Every time he swallowed, his Adam's apple bobbled in his skinny, windburned neck. He took another drink and burped loudly.

When my parents came in, Cecil and Ruby took them into the back of the house to show off a closet they'd converted to a bedroom for Roy and me. This left me alone with Chick.

"So," I sidled up to the table, scraping out a chair to sit on, "how's the farming going?" Being an only child, I was used to initiating conversation with adults. "How are the crops this year?"

Chick looked up from the crib board as if I were causing him great pain. Like Cecil, he tried to hide his baldness by growing his hair long above one ear and looping it across. It looked like grass blowing over a rock.

"You the one who plays hockey?"

"No, that must be Roy. My parents don't allow me." Which, to be honest, didn't bother me a bit. The one time I was on skates, my blade got caught in a crack in the ice, and I was whirled face first into the boards. Now I tended to gravitate to less dangerous sports. "Chess," I said, "is what I play."

Uncle Chick looked puzzled, as if he'd never heard of the game. He pried some food from between his teeth with a crib marker. "Chess," he said as if it were a word in a different language.

"I'm captain of my school's team," I explained. "I hardly ever lose."

No response from Chick.

"The secret to the game, if you're wondering," I continued, "is just that you need a little imagination and foresight." I extended my arms to illustrate the point the way my teacher had. "Just know what your opponent is up to and beat him at his own game. Or rather, let him beat himself. It's a game of strategy."

Uncle Chick swallowed, then replaced the crib marker in a different hole from where he'd gotten it. "Then you're not the one plays hockey," he said finally.

"Maybe Roy does," I said.

Uncle Chick got up to fix himself another drink. Four fingers of rye whiskey and a dribble from the water dipper. He seemed surprised, when he returned to the table, to find me still sitting there, my arms draped over the back of a chair.

"Don't you have somebody else to bother?" he said after a few minutes of silence.

"I think I'll check to see if anything of mine is left in the car."

"You do that."

Outside the rain had softened to a drizzle. It was cold and completely black except for the yard light. A car purred on the road, then two headlights danced down the drive. I'm not sure why, but I ran into the grove of poplars by the house and stood shivering as a thin, sallow woman with lank, chin-length hair got out of the passenger side and hurried into the house. The driver, a tall, crisp-looking man, got out, then turned his face back to the car. In the glare of the yard light I could see him saying something to a hunched figure in the back seat. They must have been arguing because the driver slammed the car door and strode stiffly past me into the house.

As if on cue, when the screen door to the porch closed, the hunched figure—it had to be my cousin—got out and stretched, cursing softly to himself. Tall, angular, raw-boned, if it wasn't for his adolescent features he could have passed for thirty instead of fifteen. In the yard light's silver wash his complexion reflected oily whorls of scabbed acne.

Roy yawned audibly and slumped up to the porch door, but instead of entering, he took a cigarette out of a package hidden beneath his shirt in the waistband of his jeans. He lit this and smoked quietly for a moment, staring into the trees where I stood freezing. I was quite sure he couldn't make me out in the darkness, and I had no intention of stepping into the open like a peeping Tom to introduce myself. No, I would just wait quietly. Suddenly the wind gusted and turned the leaves, showering me with icy water, and despite myself, I gasped.

Roy put out his cigarette against the sodden wall of the house and jerked open the screen door, pausing: "Hey, Four-Eyes, only queers sneak around in the bushes at night," he said in a low, confident voice. "I hate queers." He let the door slap shut.

I eased myself in behind him just as Aunt Ruby set eyes on her other favorite nephew for the first time. I wouldn't have missed this for the world. Clapping her meaty hands to her mouth—I suppose to stifle joy—she charged across the dimly lit kitchen, fuzzy slippers slipping on the linoleum. Roy tried to sidestep her, but Aunt Ruby got him in the hold she probably used when castrating calves and hugged him hard.

"Let Auntie have a good look at you." She thrust Roy out to arm's length. "I see you take after your mother's side of the family for good looks," she lied, smothering his mouth under a big, sloppy kiss.

"Oh-*ho!* What's that I smell on your breath, Mister Man?" I guess she was referring to the cigarette, but in any case she was joking. "Don't worry," she assured Roy in a raspy stage whisper the whole room could hear, "I won't tell your mother."

At that Roy broke away. "I don't give a flying fuck what you do or don't do," he said calmly. "You can all kiss my ass as far as I'm concerned."

I assumed my ears were playing tricks on me. Evidently Uncle Cecil assumed the same thing. He cleared his throat reflexively, a waxen smile on his fat face.

"You heard me right, puddle-ass," said Roy, making a kissing noise. "You even got the lips for it."

Rain pelted the window. The wind howled through some junk in the yard, banging metal against metal. A few moths fluttered around the light bulb. Finally, Roy's mother let out a gasping fishlike sob and buried her pale, drawn face into shaking hands.

The shit, as they say, hit the fan. Uncle Royce, Roy's father, flew out of his chair and lit on top of his son, driving him face-down onto the dirty linoleum, twisting his arm behind his back.

Royce yanked the arm. "I want an apology out of you, my boy!" He yanked on the arm again. Roy cried out and slapped the floor with his free hand like a professional wrestler. *"Now, Mister!"*

Roy mumbled something, then yelped again when his dad yanked the arm up still further. Aunt Irma, Roy's mother, was sobbing uncontrollably now, my mother patting her back as if she were a child. This beat the hell out of TV.

"I said apologize to your uncle—" Royce looked up, his face mauve from stress and anger, but oddly vacant. "Uncle Lloyd," he finally stammered. My father's name.

"Cecil," corrected Aunt Ruby. "Uncle *Cecil."*

"Whatever," Roy said dismissively.

"Now Roy! Are we communicating?"

Roy, much to everyone's relief, said they were and muttered that he was sorry. I don't think any of us believed him though.

"That's fine, son," said Royce in a gruff voice, not concealing the pride he felt for either his son's belligerent spirit, his own strength in controlling Roy, or both. He stood smartly and brushed himself off. "You've got to communicate with them, but you got to show them who's boss, too," he confided, jutting out his chin and glaring at the other adults. "Am I right, Roy?"

"Yes, sir," said Roy tiredly. He got slowly to his feet, rubbing his shoulder. His eyes were red from crying, but he wasn't crying any more.

When our parents left at about midnight, a knot of despair rolled up my throat and sat like an egg on the heel of my tongue. Quite honestly, my cousin scared the hell out of me, and I didn't want to be left alone with him. But, being a kid, what I wanted didn't seem to be an issue. The taillights disappeared down the drive, and Aunt Ruby and Uncle Cecil retired, leaving Chick, Roy, and me out on the step.

"You got a smoke?" Uncle Chick asked Roy.

Roy smiled, pulled the pack out of his jeans.

Chick plucked it out of his hand and slipped it into his own shirt pocket. "Kid your age shouldn't be allowed to smoke," he informed Roy.

Roy must have thought Chick was joking because he reached

to get the pack back, dipping his fingers into Chick's shirt pocket. From where I stood they looked about the same size, but Uncle Chick seemed somehow harder, tougher.

"My parents let me," Roy said. "They know I smoke."

Uncle Chick intercepted Roy's groping hand and squeezed his wrist. "That a fact?" he asked. Roy's knees were buckling from the pain, but he didn't cry out. "Well, I don't."

"You're not my dad, though."

"But he is responsible for us," I pointed out. Both Chick and Roy looked at me as if they just realized I was out there too. "But I could be wrong about that," I said.

"Same goes for you, Einstein," said my Uncle Chick, letting Roy's hand drop.

"Oh, I don't smoke," I assured him.

"That," said Chick with finality, "figures." He stepped onto the lawn and made his way through the trees to his trailer.

"Whose side you on anyway?" Roy asked when Chick was out of sight.

"Nobody's."

"Well, next time remember I like to get kissed before I get screwed." He flared his nostrils at me. "Understand, Four-Eyes?"

I shook my head.

"Well, maybe you'll understand this." Roy grabbed my shirt and flung me off the step into the wet grass. I couldn't help my eyes from welling up as the dampness soaked through my socks. "Let me give you some good advice," he said. "Get on my side fast, or you'll regret it."

With that, he spun around and stepped inside, leaving me alone to contemplate the summer that suddenly loomed long and dark as the sky itself.

The farm was by no means a thriving operation. Back of the shabby, unpainted house was a grove of bony poplars that hid Uncle Chick's trailer from sight of the main road. The trailer, a rusted Scamper camper barely large enough to turn around in, looked ready for the dump. Back of this, the poplars continued up a grassy slope to the old pumphouse which I thought at first was a dilapidated outhouse. Twice a day, I would learn, our rather marshy drinking water would be hauled out of there.

From the pumphouse, I could see the rest of the farm. To the west was the cow pasture dotted with clumps of maple, clusters of caragana, and several dozen wrecked automobiles the brothers stoneboated home for salvage work that was never done. Further out was a sparse field of wheat which, according to Uncle Chick, was usually cut wormed, heat choked, or hailed out before harvest time.

A hundred yards straight south of the well, down a hill of lush clover green quack grass and weeds, was the steep-sided dugout, an old sump pump rising out of one end of it like a horror of the deep. Stretching for half a mile south of the dugout lay the rest of the tillable land.

To the east were the buildings. Round plywood granaries that likely housed an army of rats and skunks, a barn, a chicken coop, shop and sheds, all built, apparently in a hurry, from unpeeled logs. These buildings were uniformly squat, narrow affairs with several generations of tall brown weeds and broken-down junk surging up against the foundations like polluted surf. The shingled roofs sagged slightly in the middle like horses ridden by heavy men. Everything seemed rain gray and rotting.

A couple of calves, unpenned, skirted playfully in the barn-yard, switching their short, shit-flecked tails at clouds of heavy, green manure flies while a flock of ragged chickens wandered under their hooves, occasionally stopping to peck at the dirt. In the sun by the barn door a mongrel dozed on a discarded winter coat. He lifted his head and took a weary look at the milk cows as they sauntered heavily out of the barn toward the pasture, Aunt Ruby hustling behind them, clapping her hands and hooting profanities.

For breakfast, Aunt Ruby fried up some fresh eggs in the grease from thick slices of bacon they cured themselves in a derelict upright refrigerator kept out by Chick's trailer. There was butter churned from the cream they didn't sell, and local honey so crystallized it crumbled when you touched it. Though it was delicious, all I could do was pick.

"Not hungry after all the exploring you already did this morning?" Aunt Ruby asked me. I was surprised she knew what

I'd been up to, but by the end of the summer I would realize not much got by my aunt.

"I'm fine, ma'am," I said bravely, though I detected a slight tremor in my voice.

Uncle Cecil chuckled to himself. Chick was in town selling cream to the Co-op store, and I was glad he wasn't around to add his two cents' worth.

"There's nothing to do around here," I admitted to them. "It's boring."

"Can't you and Roy play or something?" asked Aunt Ruby, blushing slightly when she realized how stupid such an idea was.

"Naw, Ruby," Uncle Cecil said, "a boy needs chores to do, right Alex?" He looked at me as if he expected verification. "We'll put you to work and you'll perk right up."

My spirits plummeted even lower at the prospect of spending my summer ankle-deep in pig shit, shoveling straw (or whatever the hell it was pigs ate), and getting chaff down my back from throwing bales.

"What do you want me to do?" I asked deflatedly.

Uncle Cecil pinched my bicep, which I knew was too small for my age, and shook his head. He groaned, got to his feet, and shuffled the first few steps to the counter, his bulky body parting the dust that swirled in a shaft of sun from the window. He emptied the drinking bucket down the sink, then went to the porch, returning with a rifle.

"It's a .22." He cupped his hand around the short, rusted barrel. "It's good for rats and gophers." He aimed out the window and in an obvious effort to arouse me said, "Bang! I'll tell you what, Alex, you carry the water—that's two times a day from the pumphouse to here, and when you carry a full pail without resting on the way, you come get me. Then I'll let you use the gun. How's that sound?"

It sounded like Pavlov and his dog to me, but patronizing or not, I had to admit it sounded pretty good too. The idea of killing things, even if only gophers or rats, appealed to me for some reason.

"Does the same deal go for me too?" Roy was standing in the doorway to the living room with only his jeans on. Though his bare torso was sickly white and mottled with zits, the power in his chest was obvious. The skin stretched over real adult muscles, and carved into his shoulder just above the T-shirt tan line was "Roy" in a tattooed dagger of dark blue ink.

"Morning, lad," said Cecil. "How'd you sleep on the chesterfield last night?" Roy refused to share the spare bed with me in our closet, and slept instead on the living room couch, which didn't bother me a bit.

Roy shrugged, walked over to the table, and took a bite out of a piece of toast. He knifed some honey out and scraped it off the blade with the back of his front teeth.

"Hey!" Ruby rebuked. "You don't eat like that around here, Roy. I'll fix you up some bacon and eggs, but use your manners, for heavensakes!"

"Not hungry," Roy said around a mouthful of food. He snatched up the pail and bolted outside, still in his bare feet.

"That boy's going to have to work a hell of a lot harder than that to win his way into my good books," said Uncle Cecil. "Cocky little prick."

Aunt Ruby shushed him. "He's going through a rough time is all. He don't know how to act." She looked out the door. "But he sure ain't shy, is he?"

We all laughed at the understatement, but before I could comment, Roy was back, the pail brim-full of dark, green water. His shoulders and arms were pumped even larger now and he was smiling broadly.

"Where's the bullets at?" he wanted to know. Then, as if he just noticed me, said, "How's it hanging, Four-Eyes?" He gave my shoulder a punch, leaving a bruise that lasted most of the summer.

While Roy spent the day out in the cow pasture shooting gophers, I moped around the house trying to find something to do. There was nothing but farm reports and news on the TV, and the reception was poor anyway. There was nothing at all to read, not even a catalog.

"The magazines are in the bathroom," Aunt Ruby said when I inquired. As if that was the only place they took time to sit down and read.

"Where is the bathroom?" I asked excitedly. In all my wandering I hadn't come across it yet, and in my nervousness anything I had to do in that department had been taken care of in the trees. I wondered what else I might have missed.

"Out back of Chick's trailer. Just follow the path behind the smoker."

I found the worn path by the old refrigerator and followed it to a small clearing where the outhouse stood. I turned the sawed-off hockey stick that pinned the door shut from the outside, and it swung open, revealing warm stinking darkness split by dusty pinstripes of sun. Inside, heavy barn flies buzzed, occasionally thumping resoundingly into the walls or disappearing down one of the two holes only to reappear crazier than ever. A barn swallow squeezed through a narrow crack in the roof, and entered a small mud nest built into a corner between the roof and wall. It really stunk in there. I peered down one of the holes and decided not to expose myself to it. I'd rather wait until September.

Bored and depressed, I took a couple of magazines back to the house and leafed through them on the porch steps, but most of the articles ended in torn-out pages. I couldn't concentrate anyway, with the sporadic reports of the .22 rousing my interest.

Finally, my curiosity got the best of me and I hiked out to the pasture, following the sound of gunfire. My intention was to sneak up on Roy, hide behind an old car or something, and watch him have fun. But before I made it that far, I noticed two gophers scurrying around a mound of fresh dirt, and decided to have some fun of my own.

I slowly picked up a flat rock, crept to within throwing distance, and when one of the gophers stood on its haunches to look at me, heaved the rock. Both gophers watched curiously as danger sailed past them and rolled harmlessly to a stop. Then their pea-sized brains must have registered fear because they bolted, colliding with each other before vanishing down their hole.

"Fucking Four-Eyes!" Roy jumped up from where he was laying, behind a stand of droop-headed weeds.

I tried to outrun him, but Roy covered about forty yards to my ten, and he had me from behind before I was close enough to the house to yell for help. He spun me around by my shoulders and leered at me.

"I thought I warned you, punk," he said. "Maybe now it'll sink in that I mean business."

I didn't even attempt to defend myself, just closed my eyes when I saw his fist cocked. A faint withering sensation passed through me as it slammed into my stomach, knocking out my wind. There was a feeble, far-off grunt, then delicately, like a lawn chair, I folded at the waist and sat back on the hardpan. Roy's toe struck my side just below the bottom rib, and I twisted into the fetal position, my glasses skittering off, smashing into a rock.

Roy, possibly afraid he might have broken them, stooped to pick them up. He cleaned the lenses with his shirttail and dropped them on my stomach.

"Lucky for you they're just scratched a little—." He paused. "Sorry, but nothing happened. Did it?"

My breath was coming back in violent wheezes, and I sensed I was near hysteria. "No," I managed between gut-wrenching sobs, "I'm OK."

"Nobody cares about you," said my cousin, "but that's good. Now you're getting wise."

When I was sure he was gone, I stood, painfully, and tried to fill my lungs. The breath rattled through the phlegm in my throat. Son of a bitch, I thought, that's what you are, a big-city sonofabitch. I might have actually said this out loud, maybe even screamed it, because I had lost complete control by then, and was crying and choking with rage. It seemed like the most natural thing in the world to throw my glasses down on the rock and grind them beneath my heel.

"What in heaven's name happened to you?" Aunt Ruby cried when I strolled into the kitchen at supper time. Both my uncles fell silent. I hadn't washed, and could feel the tight tracks tears had cut in the dust on my cheeks. My eyes must have been red and swollen.

I shook my head, checking Roy out of the corner of my eye. He was pallid, nervously picking at his fingernails with his fork. I took my glasses out of my pocket and placed them gently on the table. One arm was broken off and both lenses were scratched and chipped beyond repair.

Aunt Ruby caught her breath.

"What in hell happened?" It was Cecil this time who asked.

"Ask him," I pointed at Roy, "he knows."

"He . . . he fell off one of those old relics in the pasture. It's a real mess out there." You had to admire the prick for trying to shift the focus away from himself. Bravo, asshole, I thought. "Isn't that right, Al?" he struggled. "You fell, didn't you?"

It was chance. It just happened the way a fluky move can throw a chess game wide open. The hunter suddenly becoming the prey. I could tell by the way Uncle Cecil narrowed his vision on Roy that I had him cold if I wanted him. I had him by the short and curlies.

After a lengthy pause, I said, "Silly of me." I chuckled as if at my own clumsiness. "I was playing on the cars like Roy said, and had a nasty spill." I smiled at Roy. "I'm OK now, though."

"Was you on the Edsel or the old Valiant?" Chick wondered.

"Beats me."

"Because," Chick was talking to Cecil, "Fehr said he had a slant six motor that might fit the Valiant, so I don't want you little shits hanging around it." Fehr was a neighbor who had about ten tow-headed kids and a run-down farm similar to my uncles'.

"Never mind that now!" Aunt Ruby picked up what was left of my glasses. "What are we going to do about these, Alex?"

"That's all right," I said. "I only need them to read anyway, and I don't plan on wasting my summer reading."

Everyone agreed that was a fine idea.

I sat up to the table and ate like I'd never eaten in my life. Happily, hungrily, matching my cousin bite for bite.

As Uncle Chick was fond of saying, summer dragged like the ass-end of a worm-riddled dog. Hot, dry wind gusted constantly, the only calms coming before infrequent thunderstorms that seemed to shake the earth. Dust devils spun down the rutted drive, then wisped into nothingness. Aunt Ruby's garden grew, with the aid of irrigation, junglelike and heavy with peas, carrots, corn, beets, tomatoes, potatoes, and cukes. The crop of wheat back of the pasture changed from a rich carpet of green to shin-high stalks with bearded heads, to sparse, brittle shafts turning yellow in the sun.

Roy, for the most part, steered clear after he caused me to break my glasses. I think he had a grudging respect because I declined to turn him in, though perhaps he left me alone simply because I had something on him. In any case, while I gathered the milk cows morning and night, carted the drinking water, and helped Aunt Ruby in the garden, Roy hung more around the men. Fixing machinery, cleaning out the barn, feeding the livestock, whatever.

By the end of July, I had grown bronzed and strong. The veins in my arms wound like cord through layers of new muscle I'd developed from back-breaking labor. Then one day, under the watchful eye of Uncle Cecil, I managed to traverse the hill to the kitchen without setting the drinking bucket down. And the gun was mine.

"No fair," protested Roy. "I did it first."

"You can share," said Uncle Cecil fiercely. Roy had managed to get close to Chick somehow (I often saw them sharing cigarettes when they took a break from their work), but it appeared he had still not won his way back into Puddle Ass's good books.

"No way," said Roy, "I don't share with him."

"Goddamn rights *way*."

"It's all right," I said to my uncle. I had gotten stronger, but was still no match for Roy. And getting the shit kicked out of me for a second time held no appeal whatsoever. "It's all yours, Roy."

Roy snatched the .22 out of my hands.

"I'll help you men today," I said to Cecil. "Aunt Ruby doesn't need me."

"Hey, wait a minute." Roy handed back the rifle. "That's right, you said I could drive the tractor today."

"I said maybe," said Uncle Cecil.

And I had an insight into my cousin that dictated nearly everything else I did for the rest of the summer. Roy was selfish; he wanted whatever someone else had. So if I wanted to shoot gophers I would hint that I wanted to help the men for some dark reason. If I wanted to ditch Roy for the afternoon, I would pick up the rifle after lunch, engage in a phony power struggle over the thing, then let him take it away. It was nice to have a little force behind me.

Most days that summer, not much happened. By mid-morning it was about seventy-five degrees with a dry, dusty wind. Maybe there would be a curtain of cloud strung across the corner of the horizon offering respite for sometime in the afternoon. If I worked it right in manipulating Roy, I might take the .22 and go hunting the swallows that darted and sprayed through the trees at the back of the barn. I could never hit one of those buggers no matter how hard I aimed. The magpies, cawing raucously in the poplars, made much better targets, but the sons of bitches lit out as soon as a shot cracked.

At lunchtime, Aunt Ruby would shuffle onto the porch step and bang a spatula into a heavy frying pan. The men then materialized from whatever shadow they'd lolled around in all morning and sauntered into the house. After lunch, we repaired to the living room to watch the farm report and doze. Flax always seemed up, while wheat and barley—our primary crops—were bottoming out of the market. I doubt if my uncles realized this, though, since they seemed to be able to sleep at the drop of a hat. Turn on the TV, and they were out. And they didn't read the paper, so how could they know the market situation? Anyway, while I watched TV and Aunt Ruby did the dishes, the others stretched out on the floor and sawed logs until about two o'clock.

After the farm report came the summer tragedy report and I watched this with nail-biting interest: a family of six, fishing off Squaw Rapids, somehow managed to overturn their boat and drown not twenty-five feet from shore. A boy and his father, playing on motorcycles in a national park, collided head-on with each other. Critical condition. Closer to home, a house cat, after clawing and nipping most of the kids in the neighborhood, was determined by a vet to have rabies. Summer was strewn with casualties, and I got a small, vicarious thrill from knowing about them.

Other days were more exciting. Early in August I wandered

deep into the pasture near the end of the property and discovered a small, protected slough in a grove of willows. I was hunting gophers even though I knew they preferred to stay underground that late in the summer. I was just wandering, really. Eventually, I became aware of a storm brewing. It happens like that sometimes on the prairie. Storms sneak up on you.

The clouds were not flat-bottomed and wispy like usual. They were dark bruises that boiled toward the ground. On the upper sides bluish black columns ascended like great chimneys of smoke. Occasionally blades of darkness raced across the bromegrass from one horizon to the next. The wind picked up, rattling the branches of trees, and skeletal Russian thistles bounced by on their way to being pinned to barbwire fences.

Suddenly, silence. The prairie became a vacuum, completely still. A flock of muddy ducks lifted out of a slough in some willows, and I snuck up on it, hoping to pot a straggler. The ducks had all gone, but shaded by the bushes the slough was dark and rich with the stink of decay. I entered and squatted in the dank muck on shore as the first dull roars sounded overhead.

In the shallow water insects shot about and some strange type of minnow hovered in schools near the surface. Frogs chirruped from all sides and mosquitoes, whining high-pitched, settled over me like a jacket. Near a lily pad, no more than ten feet away, I made out a tadpole, or at least something that looked like a tadpole. It was about four inches long (the biggest game I'd seen all day), and two—this was strange—two huge frog legs protruded out of either side of its tail. It looked like a salamander with frog's legs.

"Hey, you," I said, "I'm talking to you, you goddamn freak." As if it heard me, the freak circled the lily pad and faced me, its tail swaying languidly, the useless legs pumping. "You really are a freak, aren't you?" I said. It was ugly, like something frozen in the stage between frog and tadpole. "I bet you feel pretty stupid, don't you, freak?"

I felt pretty stupid talking to it, but what nobody else knew wouldn't hurt me. I slapped at a few mosquitoes, then windmilled my arms to frighten the freak away.

It just hung there, watching.

"What do you want from me?" I asked. "Can I help it if

you're not up to par? God helps the one who helps himself, you know." Somehow a sermon seemed in order. "And the meek shall inherit the earth," I finished, exhausting my knowledge of the Good Book. "Are you meek? No?"

Heavy drops of rain started to fall, plopping into the water. "I'm going now," I said to the freak, "but I might be back."

Then, for some reason, I aimed the .22 at the water about a foot away from the freak.

"All right," I said, "if you want to meet your Maker, I'll give you to the count of five. One. Two. Three . . ." When the thing swam into my sights, I blew the shit out of it.

It was raining like crazy by the time I got out of the pasture. Lightning dashed through the clouds, followed a second later by the thunder.

Why Roy wanted to drive the tractor, I'll never know. I couldn't see the attraction to it. I suppose it might have been fun to drive one of the cabbed-in units with stereo and air-conditioning some of the larger farmers had, but all Uncle Cecil and Chick owned was a greasy old Massey whose front tires wobbled like they were about to drop off. A real relic. Still, Roy was determined to drive it. Especially after I rubbed it in that I'd been allowed to lap the field a few times while he was off some-where else.

He really got pissed off when he heard that.

"What's going on around here?" he demanded. "How come he gets to drive and I don't? He's only thirteen years old for cripesakes!"

My uncles looked at Roy, amused. It was true they kept promising to let him on the tractor (mainly to shut up his whin-ing, I suspect) and then reneged. Roy was getting screwed all right, and it was hilarious.

"I don't get it!" Roy slapped his pant legs, exasperated. "If I wasn't in this slophole right now, I'd have my learners!"

Uncle Chick, of all people, responded sympathetically to this shaky plea. Maybe because he considered the farm a slophole himself.

"OK, OK." He draped an arm over Roy's shoulder. "Don't get your shit in a knot. I only let the kid drive it about twenty feet so's I could check out how the cutters were working on the mower." He looked at me with the usual degree of disdain. "I don't know what he told you—"

I shrugged at Uncle Chick.

After lunch, Uncle Cecil and Aunt Ruby took some eggs to town, so both Roy and I went with Chick to help him replace some blades on the mower.

"You," Uncle Chick said to me, "I want you to go to the shop and bring back the big tool kit."

"Right."

"And Roy," he said, fatherly, "get up in that seat." He patted it, I suppose so Roy would know which seat he meant. "Now," said Chick, firing up the tractor, "now, as long as the clutch is in, she's in neutral. When I tell you, ease out the clutch—that'll start the blades on the mower. When I tell you to stop, push the clutch back in and they'll stop."

Roy tried it once, successfully.

"OK," Chick walked back to the mower.

Roy was in heaven sitting up on that tractor, you could just tell.

"Look at it this way," I told him as I departed for the shop, "you might not be *driving*, but sitting on it is better than nothing, right?"

The only thing I can think of that might have gone wrong is that Roy started fooling around with the gearshift. In any case, when I got back with the tool kit, the blades were clattering noisily back and forth and the tractor and mower were inching ahead.

"Whoa!" yelled Uncle Chick.

"What?" Roy swiveled in the seat. I saw his foot lift off the clutch as he turned, popping it entirely out. The tractor lurched forward, sending squawking chickens in every direction.

"I told you whoa!" Chick rolled out from under the mower holding a handful of blood. "Son of a bitch cut my finger off," he said dully. He pointed up his index finger for inspection. Blood trickled through the deep, greasy work cracks in his hand and down his wrist. The finger itself was completely off just above the middle knuckle, dangling back on a thin patch of skin.

My knees went slack. I was dizzy and shaking. Uncle Chick

didn't look so hot himself. His normally leatherish face was chalky white.

"*Fuck!*" He flung the blood into the grass and wrapped his snotty hanky around his hand. "I'm going to kill him, Alex," he said to me. It was the first time he called me that, and I couldn't help but smile.

Uncle Chick couldn't run too fast, cradling his injured hand, so even though the tractor was in low gear, it inched along well ahead of us, bucking like a scow on a sea of weeds. Roy, bouncing in the seat like a real farmer, kept looking back stupidly. I suppose he was trying to find a way to get the machine stopped, but it plowed relentlessly on, snapping off weeds as it went. The snapping halted abruptly when Roy steered over a couple of oily railroad ties partly grown over with grass and tore off the hydraulic hoses.

"*The clutch,*" Chick kept yelling as we jogged along the wake of chewed grass, mangled sticks, broken-off mower blades, and puddles of hydraulic fluid. "*Push in the fucking clutch, you ham-merhead sonofabitch!*"

Roy swerved to miss a huge barrel of rainwater that had no real business being there in the first place, and found himself heading straight for the dugout without space to maneuver. He leaped clear of the tractor just as it nosed down the steep bank into the murky water.

Lucky for him he lit running.

"See what they done to me?" Chick said when Uncle Cecil walked into the house. I had been mixing Chick stiff drink after stiff drink to dull his pain, and now his words were slurred. "I told you I didn't want no kids around. They're nothing to me."

Wordlessly, dramatically, he unraveled the clean rag I had bandaged him with and stuck his finger in the air. The severed tip looked drained as a maggot, the ragged end swollen and purple.

Cecil took his brother's hand, examining it.

"*That* hammerhead sonofabitch," I nodded toward the porch door where Roy was seated on a stool beside the deep freeze, "was the one who did it, right, Uncle Chick?"

Chick as usual ignored me.

"That's nothing," Cecil said finally, gently placing the injured hand on the table and taking out his jackknife. "We'll just nip off that bit of skin and you'll be good as new." He snapped out the blade.

"*Nip it off!*" cried Chick. "*That's my goddamn finger you're talking about there, man!*"

Uncle Cecil made it seem like Chick was being a sissy over this little thing. "Well, what do you suggest then?" he said.

"I was waiting for you to get home to drive me to the hospital is what. Jesus *Christ*."

Aunt Ruby came in with a grocery bag. She saw Chick's hand and said, "Good grief." She phoned Emergency and a minute later the half ton was on the road to town.

The next morning Uncle Cecil and I drove over to Fehr's to see if we could borrow their tractor to pull ours out of the dugout.

"What do you know for sure, Ceezil?" Fehr was stupid as a stump from what I heard. He poked his head into the cab, scrutinizing me. Like Cecil and Chick, his face was a burnt red, but unlike most people outside of institutions, his eyes were set uncommonly close to his nose. His sons, some of whom I'd seen on our brief excursions to town, had the same narrow eye-span and bewildered expression.

"I wanted to borrow your John Deere for a couple of hours, but I see you're using it," said Cecil.

The tractor was hooked by logging chains to a conical granary. Around this, Fehr's children swarmed like a pack of heathens, brandishing pitchforks and baseball bats. Their pant legs were bound at the ankle by binder twine.

"Yah," said Fehr, "weeze moving dat granary to otter side da barn." He indicated the spot. "And da boys are killing rats." He smiled at me. Something like mold coated his teeth.

"Uh-huh," Cecil said as if in response to a question, "that scatterbrained youngster from the city who's staying with us got the Massey stuck yesterday."

Both men laughed and shook their heads, and I joined in.

"What can you do?" my uncle asked. "Sometimes you just can't win for losing."

I lost track of the conversation at that point and picked up on the action around the granary. Every time it moved a few feet, huge rats streaked out from under it, bolting crazily between the legs of the kids who clubbed and stabbed erratically. When one was sufficiently beaten, someone with a pitchfork heaved the corpse on a heaping bonfire.

"Yeah," I heard Uncle Cecil saying when I turned back to the matter at hand, "he's really useless as tits on a boar, but then you could tell that from looking at him."

Fehr took off his hat and scratched at hair dead as the burnt grass along the railroad tracks. The hand scratching was missing two fingers.

"I'll borrow you my winch if you want," he offered.

Cecil said that would be wunderbar.

Driving back, I mentioned the rats to Cecil. "Those darned boys," he said. "They don't use their heads for nothing except for to hold their hair on with. Rats like that could have rabies, *anything*. But," he added thoughtfully, "that's about as close as those kids ever come to having any goddarn fun out there."

Meaning, I suppose, that he thought Roy and I were having a shit load of fun on his spread.

Actually, I was starting to have fun. The tables had turned to the point where Roy, my one-time violent oppressor, was like putty in my hands.

"I'm going gopher hunting," I said a few mornings later. Really, I had developed a penchant for frog hunting. A .22 could put a nice red blossom in the belly of a big bullfrog rather than blowing it completely apart. One minute they were harmless amphibians squatting on a water plant, croaking, and the next, spread-eagle in the muck, their little limbs splayed outward, their pure white bellies heaving a final time, their heavy-lidded eyes half-lowered in death, they looked like tiny men.

"No fair," Roy whined, "he got to use the gun yesterday."

"That's true," said Uncle Chick, who could still work though his finger (which they saved) was splinted and wrapped in gauze to the size of a banana. "Roy's turn."

"Right!" I agreed enthusiastically. "So what are you men doing this afternoon? Baling?"

Cecil nodded.

"All right! Remember the last time we went baling and all those field mice were sucked up with the swath and came out mangled?" I laughed loudly and slapped my knees.

Cecil nodded again, noncommittally.

Roy sighed. "I don't feel like hunting anyhow. There aren't any gophers out there in the first place."

And the dummy handed me the gun.

Half asleep one morning, I started up the well pump, looped the pail handle over the snout, and stepped outside. It was late August, and the sun seemed to burn from a different angle. Brilliant but not hot. The men were stoneboating cowshit out of the barn and the wind blew the manure smell up to me. In the garden, which we had been eating out of for the better part of a month, Aunt Ruby's red kerchief flitted like a cardinal among the cornstalks. A flock of geese, high overhead, flew south in a jumbled arrowhead.

As soon as I picked up the bucket, I knew something was awry. The thing just didn't balance the way it should. Though it was dark in the pumphouse, I could tell something was in the pail, slopping against the sides. Something bullet-shaped, fat, and soaked. Something hairy. I dropped the bucket and jumped outside, jamming the door shut as the thing scratched for traction, squealed, and lunged.

Adrenalin must have surged through me because I made it to the barn in record time. I knotted a strand of binder twine around each pant leg and grabbed a hayfork.

"What's going on?" Roy was chasing after me.

I gasped that there was something in the pumphouse. Possibly a rat.

Roy raced past me, picked up the .22 from the porch, sprinted up around Chick's trailer, and still beat me to the pumphouse. But, in my defense, his legs were longer, he was older, and I was winded from my run to the barn. Choking with fatigue, I plunged to the summit of the hill as he swung open the door.

Nothing but blackness.

"Where the fuck is it?" he asked accusingly. "You probably let it escape, you moron."

"No, I don't think so. It's still in there all right." I moved toward the door. The pumphouse floor was drenched from the spilled bucket. It smelled like my slough in there. Green and thick.

"Here," I said, stepping forward, "let me go. I saw it first." I stabbed the fork into the base of the pump, then hooked a tine in the handle of the pail and sent it bonging into a wall.

We heard a chirp.

Roy grabbed me by a sleeve and pulled me back. I shrugged him off with surprising ease.

"Hey, runt," he poked a rigid forefinger into my chest, "don't get fucking smart with me or I'll have to punch your head off again."

If he hadn't done that; if he hadn't bullied me just then, you never know what might have happened. But that was Roy. Dumb as a bag of hammers sometimes.

"It's me who saw it first," I said, pushing past him. "Besides, I know what to do which is more than you can say. I've seen—"

Roy threw me down, and when I focused, I was staring, literally, into the barrel of a gun.

"Get wise," Roy warned. He backed into the pumphouse, the .22 held low.

"Hey!" he yelled. "Hey *rat!*" He brandished the rifle, he yodeled.

Nothing happened.

Then Roy stamped his foot hard on the loose, rotting floorboards and a furry blur shot for the door. Rat. It took refuge in the first small place it could find: my cousin's pant leg.

Roy fell back, screaming, and the .22 went off as the rat clawed up his leg. Roy hooted and cried, slapping at the lump that inched toward his crotch. It got jammed above the knee, and I could see it reverse itself, swelling the material as it turned and started back down, no doubt scratching and biting the shit out of Roy's leg.

Uncle Cecil and Chick were at the pumphouse before I thought to call them. Aunt Ruby was clambering up the hill, her huge breasts wobbling under her sweater.

Chick unsnapped Roy's jeans, then at Roy's frantic urging—who could blame him for wanting to keep the rat away from his crotch?—reconsidered and snapped them back up. He pinned closed the pant cuff instead and Cecil grabbed the lump with a gloved hand and slit the pants.

The rat's head, snarling, foaming at the mouth, poked out.

Cecil placed the squirming animal on the grass, stepped down on it, and sawed its head off with his jackknife. Even over my cousin's hysterical sobs you could hear the blade crunch through sinew, gristle, and bone.

Blood all over his gloves and boots, Uncle Cecil picked up the head and wrapped it in his hanky. Roy had quit sobbing and rocked back and forth on the ground, clutching his knees to his chest. Aunt Ruby, whimpering a little bit herself, was on her own knees, hugging his head to her breast. The men milled about, lost. Uncle Cecil stuffed the head in his pocket.

"It came up in the water," I said.

"What?" said Uncle Cecil.

All summer it seemed I was a step or two out of sync. No matter what the situation was or what I said, nobody seemed to understand me.

"I said it came up in the water. The rat."

Aunt Ruby stood. "You dirty little sneak."

I thought she was being rather hard on Roy, given the circumstances, but then I noticed she was staring at me.

"Leave him be," said Chick tiredly. "Just let it lie, Ruby."

"I will not!" She seized my shoulders and shook me hard. "This whole time you've been playing tricks on him. Now look at what you've done. *Look!*" She pinched my cheeks and made me look at Roy who was still rocking, his mouth open wide, but noiseless, like the rat's. "You make me sick," she said.

It hit like an icy blast of water. I couldn't understand it; it wasn't fair. Far from it.

"I make *you* sick. That's a good one. You stubble-jumpers *repulse* me—"

I barely got this out before Chick slapped my mouth.

"That's your aunt you're talking to, mister," he said. Cecil was taking her down to the house, his broad hand cupping her elbow.

"I don't get it! Haven't you people been watching what's been going on all summer? Cripes, he beat me up all the time. I spent every day *in fear for my life,* but did you hear me complaining?"

Chick turned away from me, the small of his back shifting with each stride down the hill.

"I'm going to leave all you simple shits in the dust," I yelled after him. *"Simpletons. Losers."*

I suppose it was at that moment, yelling insults at my mother's brother, that I started to see it clearly—the disparity that had hung back in the shadows all summer, shading everything. The gulfs separating our perceptions of what happened must have been vast. To them, I was the bad guy because they couldn't understand the only weapons I had to fight with. There was no changing that now. Too much had happened to go back. Besides, I thought, why the hell bother?

Chick stopped and turned around as I walked over to Roy who was still weeping, looking weak and helpless with his broad shoulders hunched together, shivering.

"Don't go to him now for chrissakes," Chick said.

"I wasn't planning on it."

And I picked up the gun.

EAGLE FLIES ON FRIDAY; GREYHOUND RUNS AT DAWN

My name is Art Sweet and yours is the last heart I'll break. If you follow music, you probably heard of me. I was the young cat who stepped onto the stage at the Newport Folk Festival in 1966 and became instantly famous. I was eighteen years old and played jazz guitar with an old black sax man called Seahorse and a stand-up bass man who has since died of heroin.

The day was muggy with streaks of iron blue cloud. We were doing an upbeat version of a Leadbelly tune, and there was lots of space for my riffs so I got inventive and grooved. I played the weather, the crowd. Five hundred faces blooming in the heat, dew spots on their cheeks. I threw in some Chuck Berry, Bo Diddley, Muddy Waters. I was cooking and I knew it. There was a web of beauty winding through our sound, and it was me putting it there.

But at the end nobody clapped and I thought I was wrong, that we'd blown it. I had my eyes closed from emotion, dipped my head, and took my guitar backstage to cry. Then the afternoon exploded with whistles and applause and we were asked back for an encore. It was a peak moment for me; a high I knew I had to repeat. The band was asked back for the festival's final performance, and I ad-libbed a fifty-eight-minute instrumental which was taped and can still be heard on certain FM stations.

Afterwards Jerry Garcia of the Grateful Dead came up and shook my hand. "That was beautiful, man," he said. "That was a space altogether different from an unmoving one. Thanks for the pain."

I was touched. I was not a Dead Head but it meant a lot coming from him just the same, and I averted my eyes in pride.

"Tell me," Garcia whispered, "what is it? What happened that made you feel so deep so young? It must have been a real bum trip."

I felt unemployed because I had not suffered enough. Nothing in my youth deserved my greatness.

I lowered my head and said nothing.

That fall helping at my grandfather's farm, I lost my right hand in a hay baling accident. I had the radio cranked loud and was drumming my glove to a Stones hit when a belt took my finger and revolved my wrist around a pulley. Hand laying there like a piece of bone. It shook my heart.

It took a decade to come to grips with no hand and nearly another to learn to pick a guitar with a hook. By then, time had passed me by. Great musicians had come of age and died while I was mending: Joplin, Hendrix, Morrison. I knew I would never be the technical genius I once was on guitar, but I also knew what I had to do. I played.

In 1978 I came to this country because I wanted to play mountains. I didn't believe John Denver had said all there was to say about the Rockies. I wanted to play rock as if I was one. I came expecting to spend a few weeks and stayed on.

You see, to play something right, it's got to be inside you. I didn't know mountains the way I had to. For the longest time I played them as if they were love cupped in blossoms of stone. It amounted to protection, something Denverish, definitely not mountain, and I knew it.

I had to get it right. I stuck around. Staying power is my genius. I played.

I sold my Chevy and bought a wall tent at the Bay which I pegged down at Tunnel Mountain Campground, and I began absorbing the landscape. Call it altitude training or what you will. It got expensive so I started playing small clubs in Banff and Calgary for the cash. I was a good musician and a novelty.

At that time there weren't too many one-handed guitarists in the West. But I couldn't hold a gig because I refused to play the disco crud that people seemed to love. Maybe I wasn't a mountain, but I was above that.

I was also going broke fast, so I began playing the sidewalk folks in the evenings. It has always been easy for me to play people. I played tourists who wore full gorbie attire, which is anything pastel and a white belt. I played Yashica, Canon, Pentax; Mercedes, Peugeot, Triumph. I played stubble-jumpers with wide white eyes from staring through their brains at the horizon. I played tennis rackets, backpacks, boonie bikes. I played. Occasionally I played hippies with their police dogs and looks of disdain, but I never got much coin from them because they were local and considered *me* a gorbie.

I didn't care. I played.

I was playing the day I met Ava. I was stationed at my usual spot by the door to the tavern when she came out of the shop across the street. She wasn't looking my way, but she heard my sound and clicked her heels in time. You rarely find someone absorbed by music the way she was then. Her walk was a dance and my heart fell for her.

She jaywalked Banff Avenue and I played her. I played long brunette sprayed with buckshot stars, woodwind mouth, rubber soles. She knew what I was getting at and she loved me for it. She stopped by a pod of gorbies and dropped her address in my guitar case, written on a dollar bill.

I ceased my music, bent down, and pinched her note in my hook. I was wearing my Hawaiian shirt and smiled cool at her through my Ray Charles glasses.

Ava worked in one of the hotels as a chambermaid but was hoping for better things. I guess I fit the bill, because I picked her up one night and pedaled her to my campsite on my tandem bicycle. And she stayed.

It was a wonderful summer. We held off the world with thin canvas walls. We should have gotten a medal for that.

"Are you satisfied with our life the way it stands?" I asked Ava once. It was the first time my hand hadn't held me back from women and I needed to know. "Are we in this gig together?"

Her arms folded around my neck. "You're my rock, Art," she

said, "but do we get to move out of the tent someday?"

It was more than a human deserved and I wanted to show my gratitude. So one night as Ava slept, I wrote her song; the first of two lyrics I ever put on paper. It went:

> You sleep smooth
> in a feather of moon
> Your steady beat
> a raven's wing

The tune opened with a slow version of the Beatles's "Norwegian Wood," and gradually my fingers moved up the neck of my Gibson until they danced like flame. I would repeat the lyrics over and over about thirty-five times, in a kind of chant, creating the rhythmical impression of a bird in flight.

"I like it." Ava hugged me. "But it's a little short, don't you think?"

"It's you," I said. "You sound like that to me."

"I guess I do," she said. "If it's missing something, I guess that's my problem."

In a perfect world my story would end here, but in a perfect world I would still have two hands and be playing Carnegie Hall.

No.

On the Labor Day long weekend a cigarette salesman from Calgary camped in the site next to ours. His name was Rob something. He had a company car and dressed in sequins and boots like Hank Snow. I hated him immediately. But he heard me trying to play Tunnel Mountain and trotted over.

"Sounds great." He looked at Ava and offered her a package of Player's Light cigarettes. "There's more where that came from," he said. "Unlimited amounts."

I thought he was still talking about my music, and said, "It's quality not quantity that counts, Dad. But thanks for the compliment."

Rob just looked at me, so I stuck out my left hand and said my name, Art Sweet.

"That's interesting," Rob said. "What's your daughter's name?"

I straightened him out on Ava's status, but it didn't seem to

66

faze Rob. He was a salesman and his foot was in the door. He tried to woo me with cigarettes and Topol toothpaste, but I refused.

"I don't smoke," I said. "My lungs are my life."

"Don't give me that." Rob clapped me on the shoulder, friendly-like. "You must be putting me on, Art. Who's ever heard of a musician who doesn't smoke?"

He was right. Most musicians are extreme oral types. "I'm different." I raised my stump.

Ava was sitting on a lawn chair smoking hungrily. She liked to smoke, I think, because it made her look like Bette Davis. The glowing end of her cigarette a small wound against the mountains.

The next day Rob brought over a bottle of Scotch and got frank with me. "Let's take a look at some things," he said. "There's me. I have a good job, a savings account, retirement funds in the bank, a company car with two hundred and fifty packages of cigarettes in the trunk. I come up here on weekends and can afford to spend like a sheik. I'm a popular guy with the gals." He gave me a handsome smile and his eyes zeroed in. "Now let's take a look at yourself, Art. One hand, no cash, not a whole lot going for you futurewise, balding hair, ragged outward appearance—stop me if I'm wrong, but I don't think I'd be far off base to say you're dead weight in this world."

I blinked my eyes and felt like I was standing in a current of sewage.

"Good God, man, say something for yourself!"

I cleared my throat. "All right. I have a well-seasoned Gibson Hummingbird guitar with B. B. King's initials scratched into the finish. I have a tandem bicycle, a few golf clubs, memories of a certain night when I was on top of the world. . . . I have," I said, "Ava."

"Sure you do, but you don't deserve her."

Ava heard this and kept quiet, her cigarette a scab now, her lungs coughing.

The next day I went downtown to play the gorbies and Ava took Rob to the Hoodoos in exchange for cigarettes. When I got back, Rob's tent was gone.

"Has that walking piece of kitsch finally left?" I said.

"Don't talk. Please." Ava pulled me down onto the sleeping bag and we tried to make a song. But I couldn't. Her breath smelled of smoke and her lungs rattled.

"I'm so tired," she said, slipping off.

"Don't," I said.

When she was asleep, I dug through her purse and found two packages of cigarettes and a lighter courtesy of Player's. On the inside of a matchbook cover I discovered a Calgary address in a man's scrawl.

The bus took Ava from me. Rob did. She left a note that said:

> I love you, Art
> but Rob can get me things
> you can not.

It shook me, the loneliness of no Ava. In the night, I would roll into her emptiness and thump my stump on the gritty canvas floor, and it pained me. My lost ring finger itched, and I missed it, my hand. I tried to play mountains to take my mind off loss. For the first time since the accident I couldn't play joy. My heart hurt, and I wrote:

> My heart needs your push
> it floats weightless inside me
> I need your push
>
> Baby please come back
> baby baby please
> please

I howled this at the snow points of the sky in my Dylan voice until a guy in a green uniform drove up to my campsite and told me to quit.

"I am an artist and I'm in pain!" I said, vocalizing some wine I'd had.

"Yeah well, right, but you don't shut up, you're out of here in about three minutes, OK?"

I drank beer. I shot pool for money. I watched MTV on a bar screen. I wept. I saw an Ava on every street corner and it broke my heart. Maybe I didn't deserve her but neither did I deserve what I got.

One day, weeks later, I took a golf club up Tunnel Mountain

and drove a bucket of balls onto the golf course below. Because of the physics of height, I was driving them over a mile which isn't bad for one-handed, I think. It cheered me to watch the old gorbies scatter in their carts as God rained down on them. I was moving people with my pain, and I felt better. Like I could kill.

When I got back to the tent, I tore up Ava's song and nearly sang a mountain. I scat-sang ragged knuckles scraping sky, hard and rough. My guitar hammered a blue-black noise that was rock and anger. Rock and roll without the humor. It was very close to mountain.

In September, I was playing the street in front of the tavern and saw Ava through the window. She had cut her hair and was chain-smoking, but I knew her anyway. She was in the Balkan Restaurant which has an exquisite menu and a belly dancer of my acquaintance. Rob was there too, charming nobody.

What happened really did happen. I laid down my weary tune, walked into the Balkan, and duked down Rob. Metal is harder than bone and I cleared out some teeth. They were still in the moussaka when he raised his face to see who had done this to him. When he focused on me, I smiled big and put him to sleep. It was beautiful.

Ava's cigarette dropped out of her mouth and scorched her nice pantsuit.

I grabbed Rob's hair and pulled his face off his plate. "You tried to kill me," I said. "You tried to murder my heart."

Ava was shrieking, her fingers fluttering over her lips. I knew the bouncer by name and didn't put up a fight as he helped me out and threw me down on the sidewalk.

"You've gone too far this time, Art," he said. "We don't need your kind around here anymore."

Some people helped me up and into my guitar. I couldn't wipe the smile off my face. There was blood on my hook and it spattered when I played.
I played
golf clubs driving teacups
hammers pounding head lamps
skylights welcoming hail, I played
ships sailing back through the green necks of bottles

time splitting secrets from stone, I played
honestly because I was trying to play my heart, the sound of it
breaking. It felt right and I was cooking; the people were
moved. Gorbies dug into wallets and signed traveler's checks
over to me. Local hippies tossed quarters into my guitar case.

I played on. I strummed down the night.

I played granite snow heartbreak. I muted the strings with my
stump, strummed a curtain of stone across dreams; I did a
Chuck Berry duckwalk and hammered time into rust colors,
screams, loss.

I hook-picked. I strummed.

I played until I was drenched with sweat and felt like a
thumbtack shadow on a scarp face. Then I knew I was happen-
ing. I breathed slowly through my open mouth and began to
play in a way I never had before.

I played my heart and my heart was a mountain and I understood this was how I'd survived. I played my mountain with a
river running through and thought of the dwindling days of my
life. I'd been on a bum trip but now I was home. I had suffered
and deserved who I was. People gathered and swayed in my
pain. I was high as a kite. Not even Newport came close.

I played so true the great Hendrix would have wept, and I did
it one-handed.

When I was done, I gathered the money, placed my guitar in
its velvet holds, and snapped it away.

"Thank you, sir." A girl dabbed her eyes with a Kleenex and
touched me on the hook.

"Call me Art." I shrugged. "It's what I do."

"What was its name?"

I started walking away, then turned back. "That was 'Tunnel
Mountain Breakdown,'" I said. "It's the last song I'll ever play."

THE STORYTELLER

*W*eaver stopped alongside a yellow half ton parked on the shoulder of the road. It was still dark out and the heater was clattering, blowing icy wind against my feet and legs.

"Roll your window down," Weaver said to me.

The guy in the other truck had a gaunt face and red hair. He was pouring something out of a steel thermos and his teeth were rotted down to brown stumps.

"You seen anything this morning yet?" Weaver asked him.

He took a swallow from his big metal cup and wiped his mouth with the back of his hand. "They should start moving any time now," he said.

It was the first morning of deer season. Dawn had just come up and in the gray light you could make out snow steaming across the stubble fields in long smoky wisps. I didn't want to waste a lot of time on this guy. I wanted to get somewhere good before the deer moved off the fields into the deep bush. But it wasn't my truck or my part of the country, so what I wanted didn't much matter.

They small-talked for a few minutes about things that didn't interest me, then Weaver wished him luck and slid the truck into gear. When we pulled ahead, I looked back and saw a deep trail gouged into the snow by deer hooves. It angled in a blue strip across the stubble and crossed the road right in front of the other truck. That explained some things: it was a good game trail. He knew what he was doing.

"I've seen him out here spotting for a month," Weaver said, like he could read my mind. "He'll have his deer before noon."

Bully for him, I felt like saying, what about my deer? But instead I said, "Is that right?"

"Oh, sure. But I must admit," Weaver glanced at the rearview, "it's strange to see him hunting again. Crazy old Spivey."

I wasn't really interested. I kept my eyes on the horizon for any kind of movement that might mean game.

"Crazy old Spivey," Weaver repeated, slapping the steering wheel with his hands as though a funny thought had just popped into his mind. Then he turned solemn, and I saw his eyes check the rearview mirror again. "You can bet that wasn't coffee he was drinking. . . . It's just a damn shame."

I figured Spivey was down on his luck the way a lot of people in these farming communities were, and I let it go at that. I was more worried about myself. I'd come a long way for one day of hunting and I wanted something to take home.

At first light we spotted a handful of deer sliding single file toward a thick stand of trees. They were moving slow, pausing to look around. Weaver stopped the truck and I slid out onto the road.

"Any bucks among them?" Weaver sounded nervous, probably because it was buck-only season and it meant your rifle and a fine if you accidentally shot a doe. I guess he was worried because he didn't know me well enough to know what kind of hunter I was, and he wanted to remind me of the rules. He came from around here. He didn't need a hassle.

The lead deer had a heavy rack of antlers. Two of the smaller deer looked to be little spikes, a year or so old. I was about to pull the trigger when Weaver got out and sighted in on them with his scope. "What do you think," he asked again, "any spikes, at least?"

I didn't have a scope on my rifle, but I was pretty sure of what I was looking at.

What the hell was going on here? I didn't know, but then I really didn't know Weaver, either. He was just somebody I met at a convention. He bragged a lot about the hunting where he came from, and even though he didn't look like a hunter, he made sense. I finally talked him into inviting me on a hunt and I was hoping I hadn't made a mistake.

We stood in the frozen ruts of the road, and I thought maybe Weaver wanted to tag the big buck himself. Maybe that was why he was holding me off. It didn't matter because there would probably be other deer, but I didn't want that big rack to get away either.

The herd slid closer to the trees and Weaver moved his rifle to keep them in his scope. He was keeping me waiting for some reason. If I was on familiar ground, I would have bagged that big buck by now and had it field dressed, but there was nothing to do but wait for Weaver to make some kind of move, so I stood in my rubbers on the road, bunching my toes against the cold.

Finally Weaver lowered his rifle and looked at me.

"There's one big buck and a couple of little spikes," he whispered. He was whispering even though the deer were about three hundred yards off.

"Go ahead and take a shot," I said.

"We can't. I wish we could, but the Ramage farm is in that little bush; we'd be shooting right at it. *Damn it all!*" He ejected the shells from his rifle and got back into the truck.

I watched the line of deer disappear into the trees as if someone was leading them on a length of rope.

"How do these Ramages get their vehicles to their place?" I said. "There's no road going to that bush."

Weaver slammed his truck door. "Well, if it's not that little bush it's another one just like it."

By mid-morning the sky had lifted like an eyelid, but was overcast, the color of skim milk. We found the Ramage place in another little bush about five miles down the road when I had to watch a second herd of deer stroll into cover while Weaver apologized for his poor guiding. Apparently the Ramages posted their land and were not into killing.

We heard the occasional reports of rifles all morning, and once a fair-sized buck bounded across the grid road in front of us, exploded through the deep ditch snow and fell down.

"Stop the goddamn truck!" I yelled, jamming the clip into my rifle.

But Weaver only slowed a little. "Should we be shooting out of a vehicle?" he wondered as the deer picked itself up, leaped the barbwire fence, and was out of range in about ten great bounds.

"If it wasn't for bad luck, we'd be having no luck at all, would we?" Weaver said to me.

"If you're tired of driving," I said, "I'll take over."

"Oh no," Weaver said, "I'm OK."

After that the only deer we saw were spooked, far-off, and moving fast.

From the stories Weaver had spun when I met him, I expected to find deer all over the place out here, but I was beginning to think Weaver was just a talker. When I knocked on his door the night before, I could tell by the shock on his face that his invitation to come hunting was just drunk talk.

"You should have phoned," he said.

He went into another room and I heard him whispering to a woman, probably his wife, about me. She didn't have a clue who I was—just some strange guy standing in her kitchen with a suitcase and rifle. The only reason I wasn't embarrassed was because I'd driven over two hundred miles on Weaver's word, and I wanted something to take home.

It became clear by noon that Weaver's plan was to stick to the main roads. He said the more serious hunters like Spivey would be pushing the deer out of the bush and across the roads, but I knew he was just being lazy. Just a talker. If we were going to have any luck it would have to be on foot. But this was a problem. I doubted if old Weaver could walk half a mile in this snow even if he wanted to. He just wasn't a hunter. You could tell by looking at him. The red Skidoo suit, hunting knife, and Robin Hood hat couldn't hide it. He still looked more like a grocer than anything else, though maybe I just thought that because I knew he was a grocer. I'm a grocer myself, but I try not to look like one. That was how we met, at a grocers' convention.

"Here comes Spivey," Weaver said. The fat that drooped from the point of his chin to his chest like a frog's neck shook, and his short, plump fingers were white on the steering-wheel as Spivey's dirty yellow half ton roared past us, spraying the air with frozen mud and gravel.

"If he doesn't have his deer by now," Weaver said, "he'll soon shut her down for the day. Hunting's no good around here in the afternoon."

I knew what Weaver was hinting at, but I didn't drive all that way to sit in front of a TV and eat.

"What's the deal with this Spivey anyway?" I asked. I wanted to get Weaver talking to take his mind off food.

"Hunting accident." Weaver looked at me strangely. "He killed a guy."

I probably shouldn't have been shocked, but I was. I'd heard the stories: goose hunters moving in their blinds mistaken for coyotes by men sighting in deer rifles. It happened all the time, and sometimes I wondered what it would be like to kill a person. How could a man live with himself? I knew people who knew people who'd been in hunting accidents, but Spivey was the first I'd ever seen in the flesh.

It could happen, you could kill someone. The empty gun was always the killer. I tried not to but I finally imagined what it would be like for my gun to go off right then and blow a hole through Weaver. It could happen getting out of the truck. Or, say, if the truck hit a pothole and a shell was in the chamber, a rifle could discharge. Accidents like that happened all the time. I saw Weaver's surprised mouth, his slippery hands. And I saw myself remove his glasses and place them in his shirt pocket.

We spent a few more hours on the main roads, but didn't see anything except fat does and the occasional spike. Fence posts, leaning at odd angles, turned into deer before my eyes, and once I made Weaver stop so I could scope out what ended up being a beehive set on a pole back in the bush. That didn't make him too happy, but what the hell? I didn't know this country.

I was used to the more gentle land to the west where flatness stretched unbroken for miles, farms separated just by wire fences. Here was a ragged place. Black bushes boiled in the coulees, sharp stones broke the surface of the ground. It didn't look good for farming. It was scrubby land, recently bushed off, and roots lay twisted in the fields like black ripples breaking the snow. There was a lot of water too. Acres of slough edged by crisp yellow cattails and dead bromegrass. Where ice hadn't formed yet, mud hens flapped across the surface when Weaver and I passed by. It seemed like the kind of place a Spivey would come from, and I felt foreign to it.

In the late afternoon, we saw Spivey's truck again, bounding slowly over the hard, frozen lumps of a field, and I said to Weaver, "I guess he didn't get his deer yet either. I see he's still out here too."

"Spivey?" said Weaver, "Nothing he does could surprise me now."

"Was it a local guy he shot?"

"You could say that. It was his brother, Garold."

I couldn't think of a thing to add, so I just sat there with a dumb feeling until Weaver said, "It surprised us too. Garold was a good kid."

"How did it happen?" I said. "I mean I know how these things happen, but—"

"Stupidity, I guess. They were out by a little dugout not far from here. I guess Spivey laid down on his back for a while and all of a sudden some geese flew over. He shot from laying down and Garold stuck his head in the way." Weaver pressed the tips of his fingers against the side of his head. "Got him right behind the ear. Twelve gauge."

I saw it. I saw myself on my back, geese coming in low. Not Spivey's brother, but my own, the hat blowing off his head, the look on his face.

It started to snow in the late afternoon. Weaver put on the wipers, but the snow was thick and wet and it melted on the windshield, then froze into little beads that the wipers scraped over.

"Oh, hell," he said, "let's get us a deer."

We turned off the road and bounced along the tree row across the field to the bush where we'd seen the big buck disappear at dawn. The place Weaver had thought was Ramage's. The bush was long, but split in the middle by a narrow clearing, probably a survey line. We decided that since I was younger and wanted to, I would push the bush and Weaver would wait in the clearing for any deer to come out. I wasn't too crazy about the idea, because now I probably wouldn't get a shot, but at least I might get some meat. Weaver drove me to where the bush started, and I waited on the road until I thought he'd parked the truck and made the clearing. Then I started in.

I waded the ditch snow, crossed the barbwire, and went into the snarls of leafless trees. Out of the wind it felt quiet, like I was in a huge building. The sky was the soft gray of unpainted wood, and the snow ankle-deep and crusted.

I broke off branches, kicked snow and roots, trying to make as much noise as I could to get the deer moving in front of me. But I was careful not to trip on a buried branch or hook my rifle on a twig and shoot myself. I saw the crisscross of deer paths cutting into the snow, and in the middle of the bush I saw their beds set under the trees like shallow bowls glazed with ice and the yellow palms of leaves and pine needles. I imagined the round backs of the sleeping deer, bunched like leather gloves in the dark, their eyes communicating deer thoughts.

Then I saw them. Three of them, the big buck and two spikes. They were covered by some angled branches, their coats almost red against the black trees and white snow. I raised my rifle, but knew I couldn't shoot because Weaver was on the point and I'd be shooting at him. I wasn't too fond of Weaver, but I didn't want to shoot him either. So I shot into the ground.

The deer swept over the deadfall, through some willow breaks, their white tails flashing like candles as they disappeared toward the clearing.

I clapped my hands and yelled. I was running, lifting mounds of snow with my boots, waiting for Weaver. Why didn't he shoot? My body was starting to sweat in the Skidoo suit and my lungs were burning from the cold, but I kept running. I tried to picture Weaver with his rifle and ran faster. When I got to the clearing, he was standing there, his back turned, ejecting the shells out of his gun, bending to pick them up off the snow.

Suddenly one of the little spikes burst out of the bush behind me, zigzagged through the clearing, and stopped between Weaver and me. Weaver spun around, half falling on his knees in the snow. He snapped the old Winchester to his shoulder and I knew I was right in the scope.

"Hey!" I yelled. *"Hey, for chrissakes!"* But he didn't drop his gun right away. I didn't know what to do, so I raised my own rifle and held it on him until the deer slipped past, gliding into the trees.

Weaver eased his gun down and shook his head. "It's been one of those days, hasn't it?" He pulled the lever a few times, but all the shells were already out.

As we started slogging through the snow back to the truck, a shot sounded from the far end of the bush, and we stopped and stared silently at each other. Spivey. It had to be. I don't know how I knew it, but I did. We slogged on. It was nearly dusk, the wind had started to blow, and everything was graying in. I was trying to think of a story to justify to the guys I worked with and my wife how I'd spent over a hundred dollars and didn't even get a shot at a deer when Weaver broke my thoughts.

"The reason I didn't shoot back there was because Spivey drove by just when they came out. I would have been shooting straight at him."

I pictured it. The bullet smashing out Spivey's window, a splatter of red on his red hair, the yellow half ton nosing down the ditch and turning over.

Snow smoked across the road now as the wind picked up, and I thought of winter. Time to put on the studs, to load the trunk with shovels, bags of sand, gasoline antifreeze. You could never be too careful.

Spivey's truck passed us on the road, spraying bits of snow at the windshield. Weaver laid on the horn.

"At least somebody got what they wanted," I said.

Weaver seemed to be thinking. Then he said, "You know what the weirdest part is? He didn't die right away, Garold."

I looked at Weaver, then out the windshield at Spivey's taillights, the skiffing snow.

"He took the whole load to his head, but he didn't die. He just told Spivey to take him to see their mother."

I didn't want to see it, but I did.

Spivey running into the house, collapsing, crying that he had killed his brother. Then Garold, in the doorway, a fan of blood down his neck, standing on the kitchen mat so he wouldn't drip on the linoleum, his mouth moving slowly as if chewing silent words of pain. His mother crying over the sink. His father examining the wound, asking if there is anything he can do. Garold saying he'd just like to sit for a while and maybe have an aspirin because his head aches.

"He walked into the ambulance," said Weaver, "but he never made it to the hospital alive. Not that they could have done anything anyways."

My head traced the paths of pellets burrowing the brain like tunnels of an anthill. Pellets thrown against the bowl of the skull, glowing there like stars.

Weaver parked beside Spivey's half ton in front of the beverage room and, when we got out, I saw the big stag in the back, dumped on some straw and a flattened cardboard box. Greasy tools and machine parts lay scattered around him. His rack was so large that his head was propped up as though he was watching TV. Frozen tongue hanging out of his mouth, red and faded, his eyes drooping as if he was very tired, half-awake, or dreaming.

In the night he had lain with the females and young spikes in his oblong nest of ice, legs daintily folded.

Spivey was sitting alone, two glasses of draught on his table. I got a drink and walked around, looking at the deer skulls, jackalopes, stuffed fish, and snakes mounted on the walls until Weaver came up and clamped a hand on my shoulder.

"Spivey says you're acting like this is the first time they got the better of you," he said.

I looked at Spivey, the dirty yellow smile and thin red hair flattened by his cap, but what I saw was the stag, the brief slope of his back, loping into death.

$\mathcal{B}$ETTY LOU'S GETTING OUT TONIGHT

1. See Them Tumbling Down

Betty Lou, at fifty-nine, is too old to work in the old folk's home. Each face she sees these days is crumbling ash. Even the old guests no longer compliment her youth.

Through the smudged window she sees with absolute clarity: the residents of the home could be these trees dying slowly from the inside, revolving ring by ring away from beginnings. She pictures years unraveling like thread, whole lifetimes gathered in tufts around their ankles. Then she sees her own face framed in the filthy glass.

Nurse Betty sprays a film of Windex onto the window, pulls a red terry towel cloth from her uniform pocket, squeaks the cloud away. Streaks of blue appear and vanish like fog. Now the window is a mirror and not a mirror. Outside, thin, bark-peeled branches scratch together. A leaf flutters yellow onto the brown lawn.

Kid Colt thinks he's getting paid on commission. Crazy old coot. He spins the wheels of his chair and closes his rake over the leaf.

Betty Lou shivers. In the window she watches herself place her arms across her breast and cough. "Cold?" she whispers through two panes of glass at a man made deaf as stone.

2. Pledging Their Love to the Ground

Whisper of rubber whisking across carpet. Squeak of crutches. Shuffle of crepe-soled shoes.

Miss Applebee and Kid Colt are Betty Lou's favorites. Miss Applebee because she is a schoolmarm ancient enough to have taught most of the other guests, yet life still groans inside her. The doctors shrug in an attempt to explain the weird workings of physiology which have allowed her to outlive her time so now she can circle back for a second chance. Betty Lou likes this idea and considers it a miracle. Miss Applebee for the most part seems oblivious to it. She cries a lot. Also, adopting the worst habits of a bad student, she lurks in doorways, kicking her brittle feet at passers-by.

Nurse Betty likes Kid Colt because he is what he is. A retired accountant in whose dotage pencil and paper were replaced by toy pistol, straw hat, and whistle. He fears nothing, spurs his chair across the west wing rounding up leaves, dowagers, strays.

3. *Lonesome, but Here I'll Be Found*

Life's crazy conundrum! These years Betty Lou ponders which choices led her here and which irretrievable ones she left in the dust. Brick by brick she builds the foundation of her life: *I must have been in love. Yes. When I was nineteen, I was in love. A boy named Brian Blond as sun . . .*

In bleaker moments she envisions herself, some years down the road, simply changing rooms. Memories and collected bric-a-brac from staff facilities to guest room. Life unlived.

Brian and I rode horses into the hills. His hair blond as sun. We discovered the stone foundation of an unfinished home . . .

Betty Lou has always been old, but aside from being big-boned and having a gland problem, she still looks youngish. Sing-songy voice, girlish pigeon-toed stance, looping ponytail that crackles when combed.

4. *Drifting*

Screams down the corridor and Betty Lou steamrolls toward the commotion. Miss Applebee has been tripping people again. But she made her move on the wrong hombre when she booted the Kid's cayuse. Her slippered foot got caught in the spokes and she's splayed on the floor, a broken appliance, moaning.

Spectators shuffle across the carpet, snapping each other with static electricity.

"Somebody get the principal," Miss Applebee moans. "Don't worry," she assures the Kid, "I won't tattle."

Kid Colt looks mortified. "It was her or me," he tells Betty Lou. "One had to go."

5. *Along with the Tumbling*

For as long as she can remember, Betty Lou has loved the rodeo: the power of horse and rider; the heart-fluttering thump of freedom; those eight violent seconds of forever. Horse, rider. Two separate wills.

The rodeo is held in the hockey rink, ice covered with sawdust, sand, cow dung. Cowboys flail their free arms spastically as they're jerked and snapped at the whim of wild horses. Some hang on and some don't. One bronc rider from South Dakota pinwheels over the Plexiglas into the bleachers and an ambulance blinks into the arena.

"Let's give that cowboy a big hand," says the loudspeaker. "It's all he'll be getting today."

The crowd responds with the human wave made famous by college football fans. Betty Lou pins her popcorn between her ankles and beats her hands.

Now the riderless horse, an Appaloosa sprayed with buckskin stars, rears at his pursuers. He crow-hops backwards, hind hooves explosions of dirt. Red-chapped riders close in with lariats.

Nurse Betty is empathetic. She feels for the red-chapped riders, for the injured cowboy. But her heart is the heart of the beating horse.

Holds her breath. The stallion breaks free a final time, circles the arena, stirrups dancing, clicking the Plexiglas. At the far end, backdropped by the Skoal banner, he heaves himself onto thick hind legs, hooves pawing the air.

The humans wave.

6. *Tumbleweeds*

Seconds spilling into seconds, Kid Colt wheels off the curb.

Betty Lou watches from the window. This is as inevitable as winter. Arrowheads of geese honk and the Kid's rake becomes a shotgun. He topples out of his chair, elbows himself through the frosted grass, directs the wooden handle at the sky.

"I winged one!" Betty Lou, outside now, helps him back into his chair, out of the shattered leaves. "But I winged one!" Kid protests. "I saw it go down in the school yard yonder." He whistles for his retriever. Where is she?

At night he will slip a wool sock over the handle of the rake and hide it under his bed. He wants to kill and he doesn't want to die.

7. I'm a Lonesome

"I went to the rodeo yesterday," Betty Lou tells Miss Applebee.

"The rodeo!" Miss Applebee puts birdseed on her sill. Outside the window sparrows flutter in the dusk.

"Yes, it put me in mind of Brian."

"Brian!" Her bony fingers clutch the mirror propped on her lap. The bright cast surfaces from under her bedcovers like the stern of a sinking canoe.

"Yes, because we rode horses back into the hills one time. Remember me telling you that?" Betty Lou talks fast. She is doing Miss Applebee's hair, her hand snapping open and closed, dropping handfuls of snow. Miss Applebee whimpers a bit. "We found an old stone foundation no house had been built on. Well, of course, he proposed. Took me by complete surprise."

"Oh, yes." One of Miss Applebee's rare lucid moments. Her bowed neck is naked and wrinkled as a baby bird's.

"Don't cry, honey," Nurse Betty soothes. "It's almost all done now." Twisted tufts of white on her white shoes.

Outside birds circle. They will not land.

He proposed to me that day in the hills. . . . Betty Lou can almost feel the horse's warmth stir between her legs. *But I am myself first and foremost, am I not? I had to finish school first, didn't I?* Betty Lou tries to construct a home on the stone foundation. She sees a house similar to the one on "Bonanza," but would settle for a shack. She can't call Brian back, down the coulee, sun lighting his hair.

8. Cowboy

Guests buzz softly in separate cells of sleep. Shudders, murmurs, moans of old farmers farmed out by their children. The darkness impending outside is inside Betty Lou. The window mirrors the night, holds a reflection not quite her own. Light fills the street below.

A car stops. Driver swings out, stands blue under the streetlight. *What?* Betty Lou takes the elevator down.

The stranger is neither young nor old. His face is creased—laughter and time probably. Cock-hipped in the blue light, cigarette dangling from the corner of his mouth, he nods at Betty Lou.

She smiles demurely, imagines her fingers on the car's long sleekness. The rear fenders flare like wide wings. Must be a Cadillac. "How can I help you, Mister—?"

Ambling strides to the trunk. The stranger pops it open, reveals among other things a saddle, intricately carved. Looped over the horn is a braided rawhide quirt, a pair of silver-roweled spurs.

Betty Lou pirouettes and leans on her elbows against the wing. The car window reflects her pupils, white-rimmed planets. "Who are you?" She fingers the tiny clock brooch pinned to her breast.

The stranger stands back, spits a brown stream off to the side. His tongue bulges a wave beneath his lower lip. He extends a leathered palm. His eyes are brown as wood, no—blue as sky, no . . .

Time unbridled smudges. Betty Lou, frozen, hears a voice all whiskey and tobacco. "Sure," it purrs, "easy now."

She looks away across the street, the clipped brown lawn. The home throws its darkness from each window and her mind spins. *I am a nurse, am I not?* She feels for Kid Colt, for the likes of Miss Applebee. Her brooch beats a rapid pulse against her heart.

The stranger purrs, "Easy." Her heart pounds. *"Easy!"*

Country music trickles from the radio and the wind strokes the power lines above the street. Betty Lou focuses on the open door, the stranger's open hand, cracks filled with dubbin and dirt.

And, bent beneath a smoldering kiss the likes of which could only be dreamed, she breathes tonight deep into her lungs. Thunder inside her, horses and youth.

$\mathcal{B}$IG MACHINE

1.

$\mathcal{T}$he town is split by a static brown creek and railroad yards. When you cross the bridge from one side to the other, the creosote ties gleam blackly up from the dry marsh. Norma and Colin and the kids live on Garlic Heights in a falling-down shanty across a dusty road from the trailer park and coin-operated car wash. The Lubnickies live several blocks away in a new subdivision of stucco bungalows and split-levels on a barren, treeless crescent. Chris Lubnickie's girlfriend Noni lives with her parents in a pink wartime house close to the high school. In the fall when her father cures sausage in his backyard smoker the stench drifts down the alley, across the football field, and through open classroom windows. Everybody looks at her.

Noni spends the last months of school doodling Chris's name on her notebook covers, counting the hours until July when life begins. Maybe, if her marks are hot enough, they'll let her into cosmetology school at the Tech, but this is dreaming. When Noni isn't wishing for summer she waits impatiently for the days to drag themselves into weekends. That's when kids pack into family sedans and station wagons, cross the bridge to the A&W where Chris and some of the other blue-jacketed boys from school get into fistfights with the red-jacketed boys from the school on the Mount. Then they get somebody to pull them beer and drive to Beerbottle Flats and go drinking. Noni never has beer money since she quit babysitting. Chris usually has to lie for his. A few times he even has to steal it out of Myrtle's purse.

Murdoch went to school in Garlic Heights, but now lives in

an apartment complex on the outer rim of the Mount on a flat patch of hard, yellow prairie across the ditch from the Trans-Canada. Murdoch lays in bed at night, listens to the train of cars and semis throb down the highway.

When he was a kid, boys used to sneak into the marsh grass under the bridge and put pennies on the train tracks. The heavy wheels would squash the coins to flat copper medallions, and the boys would pound nail holes in them and string through thread which they hung around their necks. People warned they would trip the train, derail it.

Murdoch lies in bed, listening to the world hum toward its future destination, and it comes to him that that's probably why they did it and hid in the weeds, waiting for the trains to pass. Scream and twist of iron, end to the moving wheels. Who would wait for flattened pennies?

The thin walls of his apartment shake and Murdoch feels like his future is leaking away, oil from a bad gasket. If he doesn't do something about it quick, it's going to be too late. In May he tells Finch he's going to quit work at the end of summer and go to welding school. He doesn't know how to break this news to Ed Lubnickie, thinks Ed will figure he's bailing out on him. But when Lubnickie learns of it, he's thrilled: somebody following his footsteps!

"Money is going to be tight," Murdoch tells him, "rent alone is three hundred a month."

Lubnickie circles a fatherly arm around Murdoch's thick shoulders. "Give notice at your apartment. Move in with us."

2.

Chris Lubnickie can't fucking *believe* this piece of news. "This is my house too, you know—"

Ed glances over brick wrists at his son. "Where'd you dream that up?"

They are eating supper, Ed, Myrtle, Chris. Scalloped potatoes and leftover ham. Ed shovels it in like he's swallowing flame, then smacks his lips when he chews.

Chris is boiling: The last year of high school is supposed to be the best of your life, and now this? Ed can't tell if Chris is chewing his meat or if he's mouthing the word *fuck* over and over.

"What was that, son?" he says.

"Nothing!"

Chris jumps up, jostles the table. Milk slops over the rim of his glass, forming a bluish puddle. Myrtle sets her fork on her plate, watches the milk drip through the leaf crack onto the floor.

Chris towers over the seated Ed. He looks down at him, thinks he could pound the old man on top of the head if he wanted to. Ed just keeps eating. He loves Chris, but sort of wishes the little shit would try something like that. These past months as Chris's bird frame has filled out, peach fuzz sprouting along his jaw, more and more Ed has quit worrying that his son is a queer. This being replaced by: *Okay, tough guy, show me what you got* . . . Ed can't help it.

"Sit your ass back in that chair," he orders Chris. "Right now!"

Myrtle's face melts into her hands. She doesn't get it. The last few months have been one continuous flare-up between these two. Why? She can't put her finger on what's going on with Ed and Chris. How come things can't get back to the way they were? Myrtle bakes, irons, cleans—her home is in order. So how come she feels lost inside it?

She gets up and flees the table. Down the hall the bedroom door slams.

Chris slides back onto his chair, stirs food around on his plate with the blade of his knife. Ed stares at him. What a tit, he thinks, big, tough basketball player.

"You're gonna give me a goddamn ulcer or a heart attack before I get rid of you," he says.

"You can't wait to get rid of me, can you?"

"I sure as hell can't."

Not an ulcer maybe, but something. Lately there have been sparks of pain in Ed's right leg, and at work his back clicks when he bends to finish welds. It's scary. Ed's a construction man: muscle, bone. He is his body, and that can't fall apart.

Chris is washing dishes when Myrtle emerges from the bedroom, her eyes two isolated points. She picks up a tea towel, starts to dry. Ed is out in the garage working.

Chris thinks maybe an apology is in order. Especially if he wants his allowance this week. He is about to puncture the silence when Myrtle says, "You'll never guess who I saw bagging groceries at Safeway yesterday—"

Shit. Chris yawns audibly.

"—Marvin Mellon. He's making nine dollars an hour working part-time."

Well shiver me timbers.

Marvin and Chris used to be pals until Chris got his growth spurt a couple of years ago and coaches started begging him to come out for teams. Marvin tried out too, but was always the first cut. Basketball ended up being Chris's best sport; in fact, after graduation next month he plans to try out for the university team in the city. Maybe even wrangle a scholarship. He pictures old Marve ricocheting the basketball off his huge flappy feet, and tears well up in his eyes.

"Marvin told me Safeway will be hiring another bag boy in a couple of weeks," Myrtle says, "so I got you this application form—"

Chris's voice sirens: "How many times do I have to tell you that Coach won't let us work during the season? We can't miss practice!"

"I thought basketball was over," Ed booms, coming in from the garage. "What the hell season is it now?"

"Track!"

"Well I hope *Coach* plans on supporting you because I sure as hell don't." Ed, stomping his boots clean on the sheet of newspaper by the door.

"I don't know why you even had me!" Chris says so loud Myrtle is sure the neighbors can hear. She bolts down the hall again. The bedroom door slams. There are sobs.

Chris and Ed look at the carpet, Myrtle's invisible footprints. Finally, Ed swings open the basement door, descends to the rumpus room, boots clumping hollowly on the steps.

When he is gone, Chris collapses on the living room couch, palms his basketball off the floor, starts chest-passing it at the ceiling. What he'd said about work wasn't exactly true. In fact, almost everybody on the track team worked part-time. But since

Ed and Myrtle didn't have anything to do with his life, how are they supposed to know?

Work just wasn't on the agenda right now. And *bagging groceries!* What a nightmare.

3.

An empty bottle with a candle stuck in it, a stuffed Gumby he won last summer at the fair, a *Playboy* centerfold with tack holes in the corners, an inflate-o-woman that won't hold air anymore due to a party where somebody chewed a hole in it. . . .

Murdoch is pitching his life into cardboard boxes he got from Safeway. He loads a Welch's Grape Juice box with old work clothes bound for the Sally Anne, but most of the boxes are bound for the dump.

The application for welding school is spread out on the kitchen table like it's there to catch paint drips. When Murdoch walks past it, lugging a garbage bag, he averts his eyes. He has tried to figure the damn thing out. But it reads like assembly plans to some complicated machine, not questions dealing with his own past and future.

About every fifteen minutes he collapses on a chair and forces himself to stare at the form. Sweat slides down from his hairline, making clear explosions on the Formica. At about midnight he is hauling the heaping mound of sacks and boxes out back to the Dumpster. Each trip brings him face to face with why he has to move: the goddamn Camaro. Thirty-seven more payments. Plus the stereo, snowmobile, TV, gas barbecue. . . . How did he get here?—frozen in the middle of an oil-stained parking lot in the dark. The sodium lights put a bluish tint on the cars. The chain link fence, blown in with tumbleweeds, rings softly in the wind making a lonely sound. A few tumbleweeds have drifted over the fence, pinned against car bottoms. Most of the cars are new to Murdoch, the change-over of tenants here is mind-boggling. Twice in the last week he spotted two young girls roaming the lot after dark, trying handles, and he scared them off. Cassettes and tape players were reported stolen. But tonight there are no girls.

4.

The cheerleaders are having a spring tryout when Chris gets to the gym. The only teacher there is Mr. Guttenberg. This is Guttenberg's first job out of university. Back in September he palled around with the kids because he wanted to be popular, but now he no longer gives a shit. There are dark pockets under his eyes and at the moment he is having a conniption. He's trying to plan a health lesson and some kid got hold of his answer book and burned out a bunch of pages.

The cheerleaders are chanting, sneakers pounding the gym floor, but Chris sees the light coming out of Coach's office, and heads over to it. Guttenberg is seated in Coach's chair, mumbling to himself. It's all Chris can do not to laugh at the gomer.

"Goot's a fruit," he says.

Startled, Guttenberg swings around on the chair. "Out!" He jerks his thumb toward the door.

Chris sticks out his bottom lip, swings his arms like an ape. "Goot Goot Goot—"

Guttenberg pushes himself out of the chair.

Chris ducks into the hall and breaks for the gymnasium doors, the soles of his shoes squeaking on the tiles. Inside, the cheerleaders are moving their arms stiffly like semaphores. Some of them look over, but hardly miss a beat. Noni is scissoring her legs around on the balance beam.

"Hi, love." She curves her spine over the beam, making herself into a circle, her long braid slapping the floor.

Chris looks at the cheerleaders. "Hippo city or what?"

"Noni!" one of them yells. "Get him out of here."

"You have a really excellent attitude sometimes, you know that?" Noni says to Chris. She grabs her purse off the floor and laces on her Nikes. "I need a cigarette."

The elementary school next door has a ball diamond, baseball dugouts looming out of the clipped lawn. Chris and Noni quite often come here at night to be alone. Here or the graveyard.

"You'll never guess who is moving in with us," Chris says.

"Who?"

"Some motorhead Dad works with. Dad invited him to move in so he can save money for Tech."

Noni has climbed onto a swing seat. "I hope I get into Tech," she says. She kicks out her feet, moving like a pendulum. Chris feels a rush of air when she passes. The end of her cigarette glows.

"Why you started smoking is a mystery to me."

"Oh why don't you take a pill, Lubnickie?"

She pumps higher and higher. Chris just hangs there, stirs the dust with the toes of his runners.

5.

Norma's Tracy hangs out at the Husky House, a truck stop on the highway. A white-and-chrome place full of thin-legged men with big bellies and divorces under their belts. Donna Roote, Tracy's friend who is seventeen, waitresses. The truckers are good tippers. They are generous even if you don't work here. Like when Tracy twists on her stool at the counter, waiting for Donna to get off shift so they can cruise around, the truckers offer her smokes, pay for her coffee, that sort of thing. Not that Donna would charge Tracy for coffee. That was the neat thing about waitressing: you could do nice things for your friends.

Sometimes when Donna and Tracy go cruising late at night, they rip off tapes and stuff if they find somebody stupid enough to leave their car unlocked. Then they just give the stuff away to friends. It's cool.

"You are not . . . *listen to me!* . . . you are not hanging out at that truck stop anymore." Norma shakes Tracy so hard her big floppy earrings jangle. "You hear me?"

Tracy doesn't need this shit. She wishes she was at the Husky House right now where people treated you like a person.

"Do you know what they call girls like you? Do you?"

"It takes one to know one." Tracy jerks free, pulls her purse down off the fridge and gets out a smoke.

Norma watches her daughter light up. She doesn't know what her next move will be, if anything. Maybe it's not worth it any-more. Maybe it's gone too far. Not only Tracy, but Norma's boy Terry now too. They have diagnosed him as not being able to see right—he has twenty-twenty vision, but the pictures his eyes pass back to the brain aren't the same as what other people see. He needs special classes to understand this. And Colin—well, him and that damn motorcycle pack he hangs with—he's as bad as Tracy. Why doesn't he put a little effort forth? When Norma told him about Terry's special classes, he was so pissed or stoned he thought she said _glasses_. "Special glasses? Well, get them for him. They can't cost that much." But when she explained _classes_, he wasn't so sure the boy needed them.

Tracy is sagging in a chair, blowing smoke rings at the kitchen light. Actually, Norma thinks, she probably looks a lot like I did at her age. Except for the purple hair.

"You should let your hair go back to its natural color. It'd look nice."

"I don't know. Donna and I might shave our heads for summer."

"Tracy. You are not shaving your head." But hey, maybe that's not a bad idea. At least Norma wouldn't have to worry about Tracy getting knocked up for a while.

"It's none of your business what I do."

A brightness like a flashlight being shone against the roof of Norma's mouth: _Where did that come from?—getting knocked up?_ "I hope to hell you aren't pregnant!" she blurts.

"Fucking _Mom!_"

Tracy is shocked. She hasn't even slept with anybody yet and she gets accused! In a way though, it's kind of neat, Mom asking her that.

"No I'm not, OK?" Only slight belligerence in her voice. "I wouldn't want to end up like you."

"Me neither," Norma says. Whatever that might be.

6.

A construction site in the morning is a bit like a carnival. Bit by bit Lubnickie, Murdoch, and Norma help to piece it together amid the roar and clatter of diesels. In early June there is a big job—punching gas pipe under the railroad tracks out by the landfill. It is similar to the Alaska big inch, so the head office puts Lubnickie's crew on it, plus several other crews. Lubnickie is chief welder, the capper. Murdoch swamps for him: buffs, files off his slag, and whatnot. There isn't anything for Norma to do, so Finch boots her up to swamping for the staker. Lubnickie doesn't care. Staking is woman's work anyway, plus she'll be good at it. So Norma spends her days out on the garbage heap, eyeballing ditchline, hammering in laths and nails. She likes the job even though it stinks out there and they have to wear surgical masks to cut the smell.

She likes it when the ditcher gets moving, the big machine churning toward her, its wheel of claws revolving, chewing up the ribbons she nailed to the ground, splintering the laths, shattering her ears, following the path she put down.

Norma has started to dream. Maybe she has always dreamed, but if she did she never remembered. Now at odd times they flash back, bringing a weird sense of premonition or déjà vu. She remembers a dream: the ditcher moving toward her, dirt raining down off the claws as the wheel turns. She cranes her neck to see who is operating it, but can't see for the fumes, the Ferris activity of the wheel. It keeps coming, but who is at the controls?

Lubnickie doesn't dream anymore; he doesn't sleep at night. He lays in bed beside Myrtle, pain spiraling his right leg like colored wires, smoldering under the skin. He is so exhausted he walks through work like a zombie, and when he gets off his knees at the end of the day, his spine is fused solid. When he straightens, painfully, he hears a sound like walking on gravel. Then gradually it loosens and he hears clunks, like parts dropping off an old car onto the street.

He has started to watch Finch cruise around the job site in his white company car, bump cap in the rear window. Lubnickie and Finch started out together in the late fifties, back in the early days of the union. Finch, always more ambitious, was shop steward for ten years. When he bid out-of-scope and got on as a supervisor, Lubnickie couldn't believe it. He thought he knew Finch, but he didn't—what kind of a man bails out on you like that? Lubnickie has had chances to move up too, plenty of them, but that isn't his style. Now though, his spine feels like dice stacked on end, and he wonders what's in store down the line. A poster for a safety foreman job has been tacked to the bulletin board in the shop, and he is giving serious thought to bidding it on the sly. Why not?—he has the most seniority in the outfit; a perfect safety record, a bad back. . . . The cut-off date for the application looms, and Lubnickie wonders what to do.

The sun is hot. Lubnickie's denim shirt is black with sweat as if somebody dumped primer over it. He finishes a weld, drapes his stinger over the pipe, wills himself up off his knees onto the soles of his cowboy boots, and Murdoch jumps into action, buffer sawing the air. He hunches over the red scab, Ed's fresh weld, buffing off the slag, polishing the steel. Lubnickie steps back from the flying bits of hot metal, flips up his welding visor. In the heat wave distance Finch's company car jounces down the line, sending up a plume of dust. Maybe Lubnickie should just talk to Finch, hint that he wants the job. The car stops beside the staker who is standing at his tripod, eye to his transit. Finch gets out and dust blows over the car and over him as he walks down the line toward Norma.

Murdoch doesn't need sleep to dream. Hell, he dreams all the time. He dreams more than he thinks, even. For instance, it will be years before he gives any thought to the little skin cancers he'll get from working shirtless under the hot sun, in the white spatter of the arc welder. All he has on are workboots, jeans, safety goggles, a backwards hard hat. He hunches over the yellow jacket pipe, buffing Ed's welds, chips of hot slag spinning off the buffer's steel brush, sizzling on his stomach and chest, leaving bright red welts like insect bites. Ed's welds look like water lapping onto shore, perfect. Murdoch knows a good welder when he sees one, and Ed is a genius. Maybe not with acetylene, but with arc he is. At the shop they say Ed can weld the crack of dawn.

As Murdoch works he dreams, daydreams he already has his journeyman's papers. Welders are in demand all over the world. He might go to Australia, welding in one of the big mines down there. The drip drip darkness of shiny black mines, coming out after work to white sand beaches, girls laying on them, topless. One, a blonde, beckons to him: *Oil my back.* . . . No, no, Murdoch isn't into that kind of fling anymore. He is ready to settle down and the welding papers will give him the security it takes to be attractive to women. They go crazy for the sure bet, women do. To them men are like cars: they liked them reliable, solid. Hell, when Murdoch gets his papers, he'll be so solid (six-teen dollars an hour), he'll probably have to beat them off with a stick. Forget handsomeness, brains, breeding. In the long run what matters to a woman is security. So what Murdoch needs to do is fill out that goddamn application when he gets home, drop it in the mailbox.

7.

Here are the things Tracy dreams of having some day: a tiny little car to scoot around in, ten or twenty dogs—big, shaggy ones—four kids, a playhouse in the backyard for them, her own washer and dryer so she won't have to humiliate herself by haul-ing bags of laundry out in public, a garden with flowers, not food, in it, a big, huge wedding, a nice home . . .

But right now what she mostly wants is a leather skirt.

"A leather skirt?"

Tracy and Donna Roote got caught ripping off a tape deck. Donna bolted, but Tracy got caught. She digs a fingernail into a scar on the surface of the child welfare worker's desk.

"Why not?" she says. "They look OK."

The worker jots something on a form. She is doing an assess-ment, she says, a diagnostic map.

"How do you get along at home?" she asks after twenty min-utes of stupid questions.

"I don't know."

"Come on, Tracy, you've got to tell me what's going on with you if you want me to help."

"I don't."

The worker sighs, pushes the form to one side of her desk. "OK, fine."

"So do I get to stay in the shelter, or what?"

The worker just doesn't know. Her life is filled with these children: kids getting thrown out of home because their hair is too long, because they play loud music, because they are lazy. They are living under somebody else's roof and don't want to follow the rules. Something they might as well get used to because it won't change.

The worker looks at Tracy and sees about a hundred pimpled faces with mouths bent in scowls. "One night," she says. "And I'm going to talk to your parents . . ."

8.

Murdoch unloads the Camaro on one of the high school teachers, buys a '75 Chevy Nova advertised as a "mechanic's special." He has gotten rid of most of his stuff and the Nova's trunk is crammed with what remains of his worldly possessions: folded waterbed mattress, beer stein collection, stereo components, tools. He owns almost everything he needs, but there are still lots of things Murdoch wants. He wants welding papers, a girlfriend, mag wheels for the Nova. He wants unlimited good times, he wants either a leather jacket or a guitar, he wants.

9.

Chris Lubnickie is planklike on his bed, chest-passing his basketball at the ceiling, when Murdoch arrives. He hears the doorbell ring downstairs, the footrest on the La-Z-Boy creak down, Ed moan and hobble to the kitchen.

"Jesus, Myrtle, look what the dog just dragged in!"

The ball slaps into Chris's palms, and he snaps his wrists, flings it against the ceiling. Stipple dust and chalk rain down on his closed eyelids. "Six of one, half a dozen of the other," he hears Murdoch say, the motorhead. Then the talk becomes muffled, so Chris creeps quietly to the head of the stairs to listen.

"No, no," Ed is saying, "he hasn't found nothing yet."

"Even part-time work is hard to come by these days," Myrtle adds in Chris's defense.

Chris puts an index finger down his throat, gags.

Murdoch mumbles something and Ed trumpets, "Only hauling pipe! What do you mean *only?*—" Why didn't he just prod the ceiling with a broom handle? "—Any kind of job is better than a kick in the ass with a frozen boot!"

Chris wishes the basketball in his hands was his father's ass. He punts it into the ceiling.

"What the hell's going on upstairs?" Ed yells.

A good question. Stipple dust sifts down and Chris pirouettes in it, stocking feet stirring up motes.

By mid-June Murdoch has installed in the Nova a Hurst shifter, mags, air shocks, cassette deck. He is always tinkering with that damn rust bucket of a car. Often when Chris comes home from track practice or the Dubs, he stumbles over Murdoch's legs poking out from underneath, trouble light glowing above the propped-up hood.

And every time he passes Murdoch in the house he surprises himself by not flinging his basketball into that motorhead's simplistic face.

10.

Al Guttenberg doesn't get it. *Why me?* He was under the impression that his teaching contract would be renewed, but now the board notifies him by mail that he is "redundant." This just after he blows most of his savings on a used Camaro. Guttenberg is standing outside the low brick school, observing the kids running on the track. From here he can see how the land folds past the meat-packing plant, down to the railroad yards and creek where it begins to rise steeply, becoming the Mount. That's where Guttenberg went to high school—a three-sport jock. When he graduated from university he tried to land a teaching job there, but insiders had all the positions sewn up—relatives, kiss-asses, what have you. The funny part was, Guttenberg always thought he was an insider.

Coach jogs up off the track, climbs the steps, puts a hand on Guttenberg's shoulder.

"So what's the story, Al? What are you going to do?—I mean besides blowing up the board office?"

Guttenberg is supposed to smile, but he just dips his head in a shrug.

"Well, if it's any consolation, they might reconsider when they figure the fall's enrollment. I've seen it happen before."

Guttenberg looks down at the kids toiling on the track. He isn't even going to dignify that with a response. Then he says, "Aw, fuck it," and a dam in his brain bursts: He starts to say things he probably shouldn't even think. "Those motorheads, who needs them? If I see one more kid doing a wheelie on his motorcycle in front of the school at noon, I'll pound the hell out of him. Nobody does a thing about that shit. They run this school—"

Coach grins a bit, shakes his head.

"—You know what they come to gym in? Fucking jean jackets and baggy sweat pants. No color code! They don't even shower afterwards!" Words spilling out.

"I know, I know. It's a moot point. No class." Coach vaguely recalls where Guttenberg is coming from. He used to hope for more himself. He still tries to instill competitive bones in the bodies of these dead-end kids, but he really doesn't expect much of them anymore.

"—Cracking their nicotine-stained knuckles all through health class. If you leave the room for a minute, they set your books on fire." Guttenberg is rolling. "No shit, that Daymond Sawatski actually lit a spray can of mosquito repellent on fire and used it like a blowtorch on my answer book. I don't know how to handle motorheads. Where I went to school, they didn't exist."

Coach knows he should laugh or at least chuckle. It would be a way of empathizing with a bewildered young guy in pain. He should invite Goot home for barbecued steak, beers. Listen to his complaints for a few hours, pretend he cares. But something about Goot bugs him, and in truth, he doesn't care much. That's why he recommended the board let him go.

"They're just kids, friend," he says. "Confused, hey? Growing up, everything changing. They don't know the ramifications of what they're doing—even their bodies are going through changes."

"Somatypes." Guttenberg nods his head. "I agree with you, but I also guarantee you if I see that Daymond Sawatski on the street this summer I'll pound the living shit out of him."

That's it. Coach looking at an arrogant young man who has just stepped over the line. His eyes ice over. Guttenberg stares back hard, but then turns away, looks down at the track, the kids practicing.

"Well, good luck," Coach mutters.

"I got car payments . . . "

"I'm sorry."

Guttenberg's throat constricts like he wants to cry, but what he really wants is to be down on the track, running. Back in the world where they gave you ribbons for what you do and you can tell by the colors how good you are. Chris Lubnickie pounds around the track, a silver baton in his hand. That could have been Guttenberg five years ago. Running round and round as if tightening a spring.

11.

The ditcher wheel revolves slowly toward Norma, chewing the earth. She cranes her neck to see who is operating. Her ears breaking from the diesel roar. . . .

Norma sits up in bed wondering what woke her—a scream or the phone? Moon is coming in through a crack in the curtains, making tree shapes on the wall. Colin's half of the bed is empty, and it's—Norma picks up the alarm clock and groans—3:17 A.M. She lays back down, listens for Terry, but if he cried out in his sleep he's OK now. Tracy isn't here either. She's spending the night at the Youth Emergency Center.

Tonight a child-care worker came by, investigating a complaint that had been lodged against Norma when Tracy was arrested for teen burglary. The worker asked about things Norma didn't know about: interfamilial relationships, communication patterns. Then she talked about discipline and the importance of spending time with a girl like Tracy.

"I work out of town a lot," Norma said.

The worker didn't seem pleased to hear that. That wasn't good.

"What am I supposed to do? Quit and go back on welfare?"

"The world isn't an easy place," the worker informed her.

"For the love of Pete, don't you think I know that?"

This offended the worker, as if she knew everything, even what was going on inside Norma right then, which, if she did, put her one up on Norma herself. She folded Tracy's file under her arm in a snit and said if this persisted the police would be notified, the sex crimes unit.

"Sex crimes unit?" the words sounded filthy. "What the hell did Tracy tell you?"

The worker wasn't at liberty to divulge that, or at least she said she wasn't.

"Please . . ." Norma begging for information on her own life.

Now, in bed, she wishes she would have told that self-righteous bitch to go screw herself. Probably didn't even have kids of her own in the first place. Norma listens to the emptiness of the night close in around her. Where is Colin? He should bloody well be home!—him and that motorcycle. Norma works all day on the pipeline, comes home, chases after the kids, cooks, cleans. What does he do? Norma thinks of Ed, Murdoch, Rick Finch. Why couldn't she have ended up with one of them instead of a deadbeat like Colin? Sure, he was handsome, funny, intelligent, a good dancer, exciting, life of the party—but that only goes so far in the real world.

Norma closes her eyes, shuts everything out except the ditcher wheel, still revolving, churning toward her. . . .

Colin sets his Harley down on the Trans-Canada at about 3:30 A.M. on a night so clear the northern lights shimmer like the inside of a video arcade. Fortunately he has his leathers on and doesn't burn much flesh off his bones as he skids across the pavement. His black boots, though, prove to be a mixed blessing. One of the block heels catches on a crack in the road at about fifty miles per hour. Colin's leg is gripped, shaken, then set free; and he is launched. It is incredibly vivid. His brief arc over the gleaming highway, the crumpled papers and glass in the ditch, the Harley cartwheeling past him. The ditch is split by a snow fence, and there is a single power pole, and, marking the gas line that runs under the highway, a blue angle-iron post, metal sign bolted to it that reads Warning: Natural Gas. Ed probably welded that pipe. Colin misses the snowfence and power pole, but hits the angle-iron post square on, his chest slamming into it, the metal sign an ax blade in his ribs, arms and legs blowing forward, wrapping round it, his body cleaved into two almost equal halves.

This is Norma's dream.

12.

Chris Lubnickie has had a recurring dream that varies, depending on the season. During basketball season he springs above the rim to dunk the ball (crowd applauding), continues to rise, soars through the ceiling of the gym, up into the sky above

Garlic Heights where he remains suspended like a blimp, hovering over the railyards and the downtown core. During track season he is long jumping: sprints toward the pit, hits the board with an outstretched leg, takes off, clearing not only the pit but the school chain link fence, parked cars, traffic lights, sailing through the streets of Garlic Heights, zooming overtop them like a hydrofoil.

He can do anything.

He asks Ed for the Olds on Saturday night and Ed says not on your life. "Who's going to pay for the gas? I'm not a goddamn bank, you know."

Jesus, Chris thinks, he's been in a bad mood lately, even by Ed's standards. But Chris is too pissed-off to care why. He slams out of the house, immediately tangles his feet in Murdoch's legs protruding out from under the Nova.

"Sonofabitch!" Chris punches his hands through the air in frustration. Then he stops, kneels down on the driveway, peers under the Nova. "Hey, you doing anything tonight?"

The Nova has smoked-glass windows, a chrome foot gas pedal (complete with toes), a sponge steering wheel the size of a salad plate. Wrenches and screwdrivers clutter the floorboards. In the back window Murdoch has placed two wooden speakers from a cheap house stereo. Silver wire snakes out of them, loops down the back seat, along the floorboards, up the dash to the spliced, taped-together nest above Chris's knees.

Murdoch jams the Hurst shifter and the tires chirp. Chris is sucked back into the seat. His knees brush the wires and he grimaces against the electric shock he expects to receive. Once when he was a young kid he tried to hide a quarter behind the nightlight in his bedroom. The plug-in prongs burned two notches into the quarter and the shock knocked him out. Came to with Ed breathing into his mouth, a wild look in his eyes. Since then Chris has feared electricity, invisible power. But this time the only shock is not getting a shock.

Outside, houses bleed together. Murdoch downshifts for a red light, the glove compartment flops open. Empty bottles roll out from under the front seat, clink together. The naked woman air freshener snaps on a string suspended from the rearview mirror.

Murdoch plunges in the lighter. "I don't know about you, but if I don't get a beer pretty soon, I'm going to fucking die."

A dune buggy cut from a Volkswagen Beetle chassis pulls alongside Chris's window, two girls inside. Chris recognizes them as cheerleaders from the other school. Murdoch raises his eyebrows at Chris, punches the gas pedal. The Nova roars, gravel popping under the floorboards.

"Hey Lubnickie, smoke any sausages lately?" One of the girls mimes smoking a cigar big around as her mouth.

"Ask them where the action is," Murdoch says.

The girls are looking at each other, laughing. One of them circles her temple with a finger.

"Anything going on at Beerbottle tonight?" Chris asks them, though he already knows there is. He's supposed to meet Noni there later.

"So they tell me," the driver says. The light switches green and she says, "Hey, what's that smell? It's starting to reek of garlic around here." The Volks putts into the intersection, the sound of girl laughter still hanging around the Nova.

"Sweathogs," Chris informs Murdoch.

Murdoch looks straight ahead at the disappearing taillights. "I don't know . . ."

A huge bonfire throws orange sparks into the trees. Twenty or thirty kids stand around it, wrapped in blankets and sleeping bags, drinking beer and smoking. Murdoch feels too old to be at Beerbottle Flats, but since he's with Chris he figures it's OK. They picked up a case of beer, and Chris pounded a few on the drive out and was getting downright friendly, calling Murdoch "mate."

Murdoch shuts off the Nova. It sputters, gasps, then makes a few pinging noises.

"Sounds like bad preignition you got there, man," a skinny boy says over his shoulder. He is standing just out of the glow of the fire, taking a leak with one hand, holding a beer in the other.

"Well," Chris goes over to him, slaps him on the back so he pisses on his leg, "if it isn't Marvin Mellon the bag boy."

"Don't—" Marvin says.

Murdoch chuckles. "Good one, mate." He looks around. This is all right. Lots of babes anyways. "You want another beer, Chris?"

Chris twists his neck, checking for people. "Huh? I got to see a man about a dog. I'll catch you later." He takes two beers out of the case. "I'll find my own way home."

"Sure, OK, see you back there." Murdoch slumps against the Nova, watches the strangers at the fire.

The usual party things happen, but to Murdoch they are new.

Somebody starts the school song and a girl squeezes inside the circle of fire watchers, does a series of back walkovers, her long hair whipping. This inspires a short, muscular boy wearing a YMCA T-shirt to flip around in the air and do some cartwheels. Which, in turn, inspires Chris Lubnickie to attempt a somersault over the fire.

Holy Cripes, Murdoch thinks, as Chris sprints toward the fire. He launches himself over the tips of the flames, does a turn in the air, and is lost for a second in the smoke. Then he emerges, landing lightly on his feet on the other side.

Cheers and claps all around.

Shortly after this a couple of girls with shaved patches in their hair and felt marker drawings on their jean jackets start heaving their cookies all over the place. Too much lemon gin and Coke. The cute girl who had done the gymnastics earlier mothers them, cooing, "We've all been there. Don't worry about it." Murdoch was amazed by her before, but now he's in love, and drunk enough to do something about it. She catches him staring and goes over to Chris. Chris looks at Murdoch and laughs, shaking his head. Murdoch slips out of view and guzzles most of a bottle of beer, which, he pretends, makes him feel fine and comfortable.

Some jocks show up in a half ton truck, a La-Z-Boy recliner in the box. They set it beside the fire and begin to throw football blocks into it. Chris gets involved, slamming and slamming his body into the padding until it's all caved in, one side completely shredded. Then he helps to heave the chair into the flames. The jocks pile back into the half ton, roar down Beerbottle Road, back toward town.

Murdoch tries to mingle for a few more hours, but the kids

avoid him like he's a narc, so he leaves, spraying parked cars with gravel as the Nova's tires spin.

Around midnight somebody yells, "Pigs!"

Everybody panics. Beers are chugged, empties tossed into the bushes. Headlights snake slowly down Beerbottle Road. A car noses up to the fire. It isn't pigs.

"Oh brother," somebody says, and Chris looks across the fire.

Two guys in leather jackets and a woman wearing a cowboy hat get out of the car. They are, as near as Chris can tell, adults—in their early twenties. When they get close to the fire, he recognizes them, the men at least: the Sawatski brothers, Shane and Bly. He's never seen them close-up before, but he knows them. Everybody knows them. One of Bly's hands is bound with dirty gauze. The woman gets three beers out of a case, passes two back.

"Bless you, Hazel." Bly takes a swallow, then holds the bottle out in his good hand, an ugly look on his face like he got a bad beer. "I hear some asshole called Lubchuck's been saying stuff about me," he says.

Chris goes rigid. Noni looks at him. Everybody is looking at him, it feels like.

A crashing sound in the bush. Marvin Mellon comes out of the trees, zipping his fly. He spots the Sawatskis and starts back in.

"Hey, you . . . dickhead—"

The woman in the cowboy hat—Hazel—wheezes out a laugh, spraying beer suds out of her mouth.

"—You know some dude named Lubchuck?—Lubnickie or some fucking thing?"

Marvin turns, glances around. "No. Not really."

"Not really? What the fuck's that supposed to mean?"

Marvin raises an arm, points at Chris. "That's him right there."

Chris coughs into his hand. His friends have already slipped back, out of Bly's arc of vision.

"Way to go, Mellonhead." A girl flicks her cigarette at Marvin who dances awkwardly out of the way.

"What was I supposed to do?"

Bly Sawatski's eyes are bright. He saunters over to Chris, fists bobbing as though he's dancing from the waist-up. "So you're tough, are you?"

"I never said that. I never said anything—"

Sawatski circles him, staring him down. "That's not what I heard. I heard you beat up on people at the Dubs all the time."

"You're the one saying that, not me." Chris puts his hands in his pockets as if a Sawatski wouldn't hit a guy with his hands in his pockets. He wishes he was wearing glasses instead of his contacts.

Sawatski takes another swallow of beer, then, in one fluid motion, flings the bottle and kicks the air above his head with his boot. An Oriental move that hushes the crowd. The bottle shatters somewhere out in the darkness. Sawatski looks at his bandage, which is quickly pinking with blood. "They threw me out of a bar last night, so I punched a hole in the window." He looks seriously at Chris. "What's the matter, you don't believe it?"

"Why wouldn't I?" Chris has been grinning stupidly for so long now that his upper lip is glued to his front teeth. "I believe it."

Sawatski drops his jaw, dangles his arms, stares dumbly at Chris. He turns to Marvin Mellon who has been trying to edge back into the bush without being noticed. "Hey, dickhead, is he calling me a liar or is he calling me a liar?"

"He called you a greaseball," his brother Shane says, as though it's the only thought in his head.

Bly grimaces at him.

Hazel laughs again, spraying beer. A few of the boys look at her and smile, trying to win points. The girls are getting pissed-off. This whole episode, this stupid boy's stuff, is wrecking their fun. Chris couldn't agree more.

"Look," his voice a bleat, "I'm just here to party, OK?"

Sawatski starts making martial arts moves with his hands, knifing the air between Chris and himself, "Sure, OK . . ."

In the Dubs fights, everybody simply rushed together, wind-milling arms, raining weak punches down on each other's shoulders and backs. Nobody got more than a bloody nose. Chris isn't sure what he's supposed to do next.

Sawatski's fingers flick his chest. "OK for you . . ."

And he kicks Chris in the crotch.

At least he would have if Chris's reflexes weren't quick enough to cup his balls with a hand. Still, Chris goes down as if pole-axed, arms wrapped around his head.

He half expects somebody to step in, help him out, but nobody does. It's the woman in the cowboy hat who finally walks up to him, and that is to kick him in the ribs with her pointy-toed boots.

"I hate it when they turtle on you," she says to the world at large. She kicks him again. Then the three of them get back in the car, taillights disappearing down the winding road.

13.

Colin's Harley turns onto the parched lawn, sputters to silence. Norma is sitting on the chesterfield, watching TV. She stretches her neck to see out the front window. Terry walks past. Norma gets up, goes to the screen door, stands behind it, arms crossed. Colin is kneeling beside the bike, adjusting something. He ruffles Terry's hair, strides back on the Harley, starts it up. It coughs a few times, then runs rough. Colin shuts it off, kneels beside it again. This time when he kicks it over, it purrs. He reaches out, ruffles Terry's hair again, and Terry just stands there grinning like he has witnessed a miracle. Colin tosses him the spare helmet and Terry buckles it on, gets behind him.

Norma is out the door, leaning off the step. "Where are you two going?"

Colin is fiddling his boot on the gearshift or something. He glances up, blank look on his face. "I thought you were at work." His right wrist twists slightly with each wave of the motor, cords on his arm standing out. Temporary Manpower hired him to clean up a grain spill in the railyards, so he's been getting up before Norma these past few mornings. His back is killing him from the shoveling, but he has a couple of hundred hard-earned bucks in his pocket, plus the job is finished. Welfare loves him, the railway loves him, the mice he didn't hammer to shit when he found them in the grain love him, he loves himself for accomplishing something, and he can sleep in tomorrow.

"Well I'm not," Norma says.

"I see that."

"It's our EDO."

Colin looks back at Terry who is busy examining whatever he just picked out of his nose. "Her what? What did she say?"

"I said EDO."

"Ego?"

"Ha-ha. Earned Day Off. I thought we could do something this afternoon. Go to the mall or something."

"I don't know, babe, sounds like too much fun to me." Colin shuts down the Harley. "What do you say, buckshot?" he says to Terry, who is now absorbed by some insect buzzing around the bike.

"You know, I think we should let Tracy go to military camp if she wants to," Norma says.

They are in Zellers's coffee shop, a cart beside them full of purchases: checkered tea towels, fuzzy new bath mat and toilet seat cover, metal clothes hooks, flowered pillow cases, and a pair of black, bulbous, low-cut running shoes Norma bought for Terry for $12.98 plus tax. She almost had the boy in tears, making him try them on, and Colin can understand why, ugly fucking things.

He's appalled, all this shit. Norma spent almost as much as he made in two days of work on cheap, stupid junk.

"I think so too," he says, though this is another thing that confuses Colin—Tracy liking the military?

Norma made her join the militia as soon as she was old enough, thinking the discipline would do the kid good. Colin hates uniforms, pigeons, "M*A*S*H" on TV, but he had to agree about the discipline part, so he let Norma enlist his daughter. Lo and behold if Tracy didn't like it. Hell, she loved it, everything about it: the itchy duck uniform, the beret, the shiny lace-up army boots. Jesus.

"And what about Terry's classes?" Norma says. She is licking an ice cream cone.

Colin looks at Terry, who is in his never-never world again.

"Sign him up."

"Colin!"

"Hey champ," Colin pinches his son's biceps, and Terry

smiles, his teeth brown from chocolate ice cream, "how you doing, huh? That ice cream taste as good as it looks?"

Terry nods.

"No, seriously," Colin says to Norma, "I was wrong about the classes. If they'll help, do it." Norma has on makeup, rouge on her cheeks, little touch-ups here and there. Colin grins at her. "So you should get these EDOs more often."

"Actually," Norma scoots her elbows forward on the table, her voice an excited whisper, "this might be my last one. I might be getting a promotion, going out-of-scope—"

"What the hell does that mean?"

"Out of the union," Norma says, like Colin ought to know that. "I probably shouldn't say anything about it till I know for sure—"

"Hey, I'm your husband—"

"OK, there is a safety foreman job open, and they said if nobody with seniority bids it, I could have it for a ninety-day trial. I said I don't know anything about safety, but they said, it's all by the book, so . . ."

Colin listens to his wife drone on. By the book, she says. She has changed so much he probably understands the world Terry inhabits better than the one Norma is coming from. Safety foreman? Norma? Colin's never been more than a grunt in his entire life. He hates work, careers. There's never been a foreman he could stomach, and now he's about to be married to one.

14.

The last days of June are climactic. Chris wins several ribbons at a big track-and-field meet, is awarded a special pin by the principal, is on the cover of the school yearbook. At spring commencement he and some other jocks mimic a heavy metal band on stage by wearing body stockings, rubber boots, and mops on their heads. It's a hoot.

A few days before the end of June, he bumps into Coach in the biology lab. Coach teaches bugs on the side. It's hilarious to see him in a sports coat talking about order, family, genus, species, when it's obvious he'd rather be passing a ball around the lab, smashing test tubes and bead balances.

"So what are your plans for next year?" he asks Chris.

"Plans?"

"Seriously, though, what are they?"

There is a vague notion of university, but this hinges on a basketball scholarship. Ed has made it clear to Chris that he and Myrtle aren't going to help. "Nobody helped me and I made out fine," is Ed's reasoning. Also: You don't respect anything you get for nothing. He wants Chris to find a job.

"I'm going to the university basketball camp," Chris says. "After that, who knows?"

Coach looks surprised to hear this. "Really? Well, you were a hell of a point guard." He pats Chris on the back like he's sending him into a tough game. "Let me know how things work out, will you?" Turns back to some tests he is marking.

"I will."

Guttenberg is alone in the gym office, nose in a file folder. Chris has to stand in the doorway a full minute before he gets noticed.

"What are you hanging around here for?" Guttenberg slaps the folder shut.

Chris protrudes his lower lip. "Goot's a hoot," he says. He flops down in Coach's chair.

"Get your ass out of here. I mean it."

"Lighten up, Goot." Chris picks a pencil up off Coach's desk, clenches it between his teeth, and studies the various team pictures tacked to the walls. His grinning mug is in most of them and Chris marvels at how little he has changed over four years.

A group of freshmen burst out of the locker room and troop past the gym office in shorts, holding football helmets by their facemasks. When they are out of sight of the door, Chris knows what they're doing from memory: shoving each other into the walls.

He shakes his head, yawns. "Summer practice, eh Gooter? I'm glad those days are over for me."

Guttenberg zips his blue sweat jacket. "I'm going to have to ask you to quit with the musings and uproot yourself." He hangs a stopwatch around his neck. "Now. Today."

Chris reclines in Coach's chair, rests his feet on the desk. "Go ahead, Coach knows I'm here."

A ridge of tension pops out along Guttenberg's jaw as if he is grinding his teeth. He clicks the door closed and leans against it.

"You know, Goot, I never did ask you how you like our little school." On a sheet of foolscap, Chris prints in blocky letters, large enough for Guttenberg to see:

EVALUATION

He poises the pencil over the foolscap.

"I'll like it a lot more when you're gone," Guttenberg says stiffly, thinking, but I'll like it even better when I'm gone. "Now are you going to leave or am I going to throw you out?"

"Scary monsters," Chris says in mock horror. "You wouldn't use violence on a student, would you, Goot?"

"I would, but you'd probably turtle on me."

Chris laughs. What? Is it all over the school? "Goot Goot Goot." He crumples the foolscap, scores a bucket in the garbage can in the corner of the room. He pretends nothing is wrong, but when he gets outside, he punches the wall.

15.

For grad one friend gets a paid European vacation. Another walks out one morning to find a shiny new MG sports car in the driveway. Most of Chris's friends—jocks—are from well-off families, but even Noni, whose parents are chintzy immigrants, gets an expensive 35 millimeter camera. Chris wakes up the morning of the graduation ceremony to find two boxes on the kitchen table. One contains a pair of steel-toed ox-blood Kodiak work boots arranged yin-yang in white tissue paper. The other is a soft-sided suitcase that folds open so you can hang clothes inside.

Ed's already been at work for an hour and a half by the time Chris gets up, but he drives home to watch Chris tear off the paper. He is a father who never misses an occasion: used to hide stained eggs for Chris at Easter time; doles out Halloween candy to the neighborhood kids; shoots his own Thanksgiving goose; Christmas, he says every year, is for the children.

When he comes in the front door Chris is at the kitchen table, head in his hands. One of the Kodiaks is on the floor by the stove. Myrtle is at the sink, looking out at Ed's rig parked in the driveway.

"Mother," Ed is rather puzzled, "did you tell him about what's in the pocket of the suitcase?"

Chris perks up. He almost knocks his plate on the floor, scrambling to unzip the pocket . . . a travel alarm clock in a leatherette shell.

"There's one more thing," Ed says.

Chris moans.

"I—how should I put this—I pulled some strings at work and got you a job starting July three. You'll be working for electrical up in the city, apprentice lineman on construction. Ten-, twelve-hour days, $6.83 an hour to start, but you won't be spending your paycheck because . . . where's he going, mother?"

Chris gets up shakily from the table, starts for the stairs, the world of work on his back like an anvil. He's going upstairs to lie down for a couple of years.

"Son—"

Chris whirls. "Shut up!" He swipes the travel bag off the table, kicks it across the floor into the refrigerator.

Ed is stunned; truly baffled. He looks at Myrtle.

"What about basketball camp!" Chris cries. "Why doesn't anybody ever listen to me around here?"

"Goddamn it, boy! Nothing's good enough for you, is it? I went out on a limb to get you this job."

Myrtle covers her mouth. She knows Ed talked to Rick Finch about Chris. That had to be hard.

"There was a list of four hundred names ahead of yours you goddamn big tit—" Ed talking fast, face red as a beet, waving his fists.

Chris puts his head down and charges his father. He catches Ed with a shoulder, drives him off his cowboy boots onto the table, skids it across the floor, plates frizbeeing everywhere, toast putting off-white stains on the walls. Ed twists one boot onto the floor, hooks a punch at his son's head. Chris ducks it, scoots under the arm, comes up behind Ed, pops him in the back of the head with his knuckles. Ed spins away, they face each other, breathing hard. Chris knows Ed won't hurt him, not really, so he isn't afraid. Myrtle has vanished. There are sobs coming from the bedroom.

"I'm done," Ed says, a spike of pain in his spine.

"I'm done with *you*."

Outside, Murdoch is sitting in Ed's rig, the rig they fabricated together last winter, watching the figures move in and out of the frame of the kitchen window. He knows Ed as well as he knows himself. He doesn't want to know what's going on.

RUMORS OF FOOT

*T*wenty years without direct word, and then, out of the blue, a phone call.

"I need you, Bud."

I rested the receiver against my chest. What do you tell a man whose dreams you betrayed in the bursting seconds of youth? How do you answer for something like that?

"Where," I said, "and when?"

Hours later I'm flying. My wife, alone in the terminal, a confused citizen of my life. I am up in the air, returning to regain something.

Memory
serves like a tennis pro acing a tea cup. You'll never make a clean return, and if you try you will be struck by shards of the past, and it will hurt. Still, there are times when the world feels like a baseball in your palm. You can do anything. That's how I felt: there was a feeling inside that had been gone a long, long time.

Foot and Buddy, Buddy and Foot. Left wing and center, forward and guard. God, we were good. Baseball, whacking home runs into backyards. Hockey, slapshots ringing off the goalposts, snicking the net. Basketball, dominating the boards over tall, thin boys with change purse collarbones and futures in the college ranks. Football . . .

But let me tell you about Foot Rose. He was the dreamer and the dream, the champion of desire, the harbinger of youth. Truly a beautiful man. He paid a price along the way—he lost some things. But he didn't lose me, not in spirit he didn't. I don't care what the rumors say because I loved the Foot. I always will.

Rumors

Nobody knows where they come from. Origin unknown. But they descend on us and we gather, pass them around like photographs.

"Did you hear the latest on Wonder Boy?"

"Do tell."

"Well, apparently he's jogging on the Great Chinese Wall."

"The Wall of China? No!"

"This is what I understand. On top of it yet. Not getting paid a red penny, either."

"Oh," tucking a loop of fat under the belt, "of course not."

"Sounds like vintage Foot to me."

"Foot Rose is Foot Rose, etcetera and so on."

"Always was, always will be. Won't never grow up."

I admit it, we in his hometown mocked him. But, you see, when all you have left are the diminished dreams of middling health, early retirement, and peaceful, faraway death, you hold onto these hard. Foot was something gone in us now, and I guess we were jealous. But I know we waited for those rumors like the rest of a song heard passing beneath a bridge.

Foot Rose skiing the spine of the Alps.
Playing semi pro soccer in Brazil, drinking with Pele.
Pacing Sherpas up Everest's stone-studded slopes.

The plane set down in a city to the south where drooping cedars leaned across streets, touched their leaves like old friends shaking hands. It was a place of ancient frame houses, snapping flags, humidity. I taxied to Foot's address and stood on the street in front of a motor home raised up on blocks.

As the taxi pulled away, I bent for my bags, and a scab-colored station wagon with half-moons of rust above the wheels swerved around the corner and nearly hit me. It could have killed me, but it didn't stop. Several gap-toothed youngsters laughed at me through the smudged rear window as the car roared away.

Football

Last day of the season, last year of high school. Late October, late afternoon. Field blue and hard as a sheet of steel, snow smoking across it. My feet are hammerheads welded to my ankles; I hobble when I run.

Hard to believe, but we are losing. Down by two. Third and ten from our own forty. Barring penalty, the last play of the game. I search the sidelines for a call and see Coach fling his clipboard in the air. We huddle, helmets clicking together. Some of us are crying, eyes blue chips of ice. I can't throw into this wind and I implore my men to forgive me for what I'm about to do: sink to one knee behind a horseshoe of linemen, wait for the gun. Slump off the field, back to school, and, in a few months, into adulthood.

"Don't quit on me," Foot whispers into my earhole. "Let me try a field goal."

On the sidelines, Coach was exploding his arms. We had never resorted to a field goal before. On the other hand, Foot was our kick-off man. I made a split-second decision, the correct one. Punt formation. I knelt on the snow, *barked the cadence, there was the watch on the referee's blue wrist, the ball wobbling from between the center's legs crisp as a frozen bleach bottle in my hands . . .*

The motor home was locked, but from behind it I heard a strange rhythmical breathing. I rounded the rear bumper and saw what can only be described as an old woman on a padded bench, straining beneath a barbell. Her breath shattered from false teeth and she had on nylon running shorts, Nike shoes, a mesh tank top that flapped on her bones like a flag. She placed the barbell in the bench's metal palms and sat up.

"You must be Buddy," she said. "From what I heard about you, I'm surprised you kept your word."

Memories (of the kick)

A single piston sparking life in a machine that would never stop. A missile bursting the skin of the sea, losing itself in space. My head exploding.

Where was the ball? We gawked at the sky. Then, there—a

flake of ash in the wind over the hash marks, arcing down between the uprights, burying itself in an end zone snowdrift. *Eighty yards,* I remember thinking, *not even George Blanda . . .*

The old woman's name was Ma Bird. She told me Foot was at the stadium and jabbed the barbell in its direction.

When had I begun to grow old? Not long after that football game, I guess. A cheerleader placed a hammerlock on my heart, and there was a weird security in losing some freedom. Her name was Maureen and she made me quit hockey for my teeth. I took to sitting around with her. Got a part-time job, put my money into a car. Maureen made me give up basketball because she said my knees looked like a chicken's. Badminton, she said, was fey. So I threw everything away and more or less started to become what I thought was a man.

Foot, meanwhile, was becoming famous. *Sports Illustrated* got wind of the eighty-yarder and published his photo in their "Look Out" section above a five-year-old pool shark who shot a perfect game of snooker, wheeling himself around the table on a castered office chair. Scholarship offers poured in.

The stadium lifted out of the trees and homes like a volcanic cone. Inside was emptiness, but I heard a ticking sound and followed it around until I spotted the distant back of a runner pounding up the end zone steps. When I got close, I could see the hamstrings bulge, arms shoot forward and back, muscles rippling like heavy ropes making shapes under the skin like wishbones. At the crest, Foot turned, and time flaked away like cells of dead skin. He hadn't changed at all. We raced toward each other and embraced like guys.

In June, Foot took me into the locker room and said he was getting a lot of good scholarship offers. I told him I suspected as much and that he deserved them.

"What I'm saying is, we're a team. If anybody gets me, you get a free ride too."

"Me?" I said. "Why?"

"Foot and Buddy, Buddy and Foot," Foot said. "Because you were there—"

I knew what he meant, that I'd been there all along, but things were different now. I made a face and waved my hand as if to frighten off smoke. "So were a lot of other people there," I said.

"You pinned the ball, though."

"I have my own life," I said. "Let me live it."

A few days later Foot hauled me away from a crowd of smokers in front of the school and asked me to jog a few laps with him. We were side by side for a few moments, then my lungs started scratching, my feet clumping. Pretty soon Foot's back was disappearing. I hobbled to the showers.

I was toweling off when Foot clacked in wearing his cleats.

"Pin some for me?" he asked.

Water dripped from the sag of my belly. "I'm getting married," I said. "Maureen and me."

"You and *Submarine*?"

"I'd be proud if you'd be my best man."

"What about football, though?"

"What about it? Football's over."

"When?"

"Now! Forever!"

Foot swung open his locker and held a sheaf of papers. "Washington State," he said dully. "The Crimson Tide." He was licking his thumb and flinging the papers one by one into the water at my feet, his scholarship offers becoming diaphanous on the floor. We stood ankle-deep in a stack of dream places. "Clemson, Boston College, Miami of Florida, Cornhuskers, Oklahoma Sooners . . ." He could have gone on and on, but he just pitched the remaining pages down and clacked out of the locker room and out of my life. He didn't write his final exams, so he blew his chances for college. The rumors have him burning his cleats in a trash barrel outside the bus depot, leaving town.

But you can't trust rumors.

The motor home was a mausoleum for old athletes. Photos of Gordie Howe, Muhammad Ali, Tony Esposito, Wilt Chamberlain, Phil Niekro. Above the sit-up ramp, a blow-up of George Blanda, his boot cleat lifting a small clump of lawn, hands thrown up as if describing the size of a fish. Somewhere off-camera, the ball splitting the uprights.

Foot revved the blender, began ramming fruit in. He measured out a portion of odious powder and poured everything into an empty peanut butter jar.

"So, what's Submarine say about you coming?" He was sipping from the jar.

"She wasn't too happy."

Foot looked pleased. "You did the honorable thing," he said. "This time."

I followed Foot to the window and we looked outside. The old weightlifter from that afternoon was coiling herself into painful yogalike positions on the grass.

"Sixty-eight years old," Foot said in a tone that indicated amazement. "Can you believe it?"

She looked to me like a child wearing a soiled body stocking and a fright mask; every second of sixty-eight. Her moans were audible through the glass.

"We met on a jogging trail," Foot said. "She's my old lady."

I pictured Foot and the old woman together. Then I tried not to, but couldn't.

"She moved in right away and we decided we'd band together and push for my dream. Now or never was the way we looked at it."

"Your dream?" I said.

Ma Bird

Foot told me her story. This is it: A few years before, she and her husband retired and headed south. Before they made a hundred miles, a tire on the motor home blew. Ma's husband pranced out, jacked up the vehicle, cranked on the spare, and had a heart attack. He passed away right there on the shoulder of the road. Ma must have been a naive old woman because when she saw him lying there like a stick, her eyes opened on death for the first time. She was furious. You trust your future with a guy and he dies on you. Since there was no one else, she fed him into the local incinerator, pointed the motor home down the road.

Foot's Dream
was to play football.

"No team would look at a guy your age," I said.

"Just tell me if you're with me or not."

"Come on, Foot! You might be in good shape, but you're still how old you are. Those college kids would shatter your bones!"

"Not college," Foot said, "pro."

"Pro!"

"Just give me tomorrow, Buddy. Give me a chance is all I ask. If I don't measure up after that, you walk away guilt-free."

What could I say? We watched Ma Bird's luminous running shoes wobble into the night, moving down the street where traffic loomed and tires screamed.

I didn't sleep until dawn. All night I lay cramped on the couch listening to Foot and Ma sleep like an audience of clapping hands. It was a weird picture, believe me. Finally I drifted into a dream of myself and Maureen.

"Pin it."

I am on the fifteen yard line. This is pathetic, a lineman could kick a field goal from here. Solemnly Foot strides toward the uprights, swiping bits of paper out of his path with the toe of his cleat. When he turns to look at me, I can't meet his eyes. It's that embarrassing.

"You're on the wrong side," Foot says.

I look up. Foot is pointing at the other uprights. From where I'm kneeling they look like a tuning fork. Gulls whirling over them are just specks on my glasses. Foot moving toward me, a blur.

Here, abridged, is my diary of the next several weeks:

Arise at dawn. Foot climbs five miles of stadium steps.

Noon: Kicks one thousand field goals (I learned to handle the balls like cobs of corn, setting them down with factory exactness). Ma Bird, in the end zone, shags the balls, sprints them back. Longest stretch without a miss: three weeks.

Evenings: pasta, vitamins, protein drink, cool down with a

street game of aerial football, crowd noise simulated by traffic hums. (Twice a week phone Maureen—don't let Foot know about this).

In early May we are ready. Take the motor home down off the blocks, hit the road.

Recounting the rest is like explaining dream logic. It doesn't make sense. Suffice it to say nobody wanted an aging free agent with no college experience in their training camp.

Team after team, city after city, the same. Ma rubs Foot down with antiphlogistic, sends him out with the other boys fighting for a kicking job.

"Who's that geezer?" one of them would say.

"Kind of looks like Tab Hunter."

"Yeah? Who's Tab Hunter?"

A team lackey would putt out in a golf cart.

"I'm Foot Rose. I'm a free agent," Foot would explain.

"You'll have to leave, irregardless, sir."

"Why?"

"Medical reasons."

"I'm fit as a fiddle, though."

"It's out of my hands. We're not covered."

At first we chuckled it off, got psyched for the next camp, but time made Foot angry. In Cincinnati, he had to be forcibly removed from the playing surface by security officers, two linemen, Ma Bird, and myself. He didn't even get a chance to warm up.

It wasn't fair. Here was possibly the greatest leg of all time, a man with reckless ability and the heart of a child. But the world wouldn't let him play.

Depression banked up. Twenty towns, twenty rejections.

One night, feeling snarly, we unwound with a game of street football. It was dark, there was too much traffic, we shouldn't have played. I have nothing more to say about it.

The next day our luck changed. When they told Foot to leave the field, he saw a ball cupped in a plastic tee in front of the warm-up net which looked a bit like a wall of nylon mesh. He took a step toward it, blasted through an oblong hole.

The peak of the head coach's cap flipped up and the aluminum frame of the warm-up net folded in a kind of curtsy to the ground. The lackey who'd sent Foot away U-turned his cart midfield. But the reporters were already there.

Foot kicked ten field goals in three preseason games. After he single-handedly defeated Chicago, Jim McMahon joked on "Letterman" that oldsters shouldn't be allowed to play in the NFL.

There is a "60 Minutes" piece that ends with two child actors, one pinning a football, the other kicking in a cinder schoolyard. This is superimposed by myself pinning for Foot on the practice field, once again being superimposed by actual game footage of Foot's five field goals against the Bears.

As Foot is being slow-motion swarmed by his teammates, Diane Sawyer recites:

> and dreaming just comes natural
> like the first breath from a baby
> like sunshine feeding daisies
> like the love hidden deep in your heart

and my face superimposes the everyman in the crowd.

The dream
died somewhere along the way. Foot suggested a game of street football. We were wired, tense. It seemed like a good idea. Foot defended Ma. I was quarterback. The ball went deep on a post pattern at the same instant back-up lights flicked on in a driveway. Ma went up for the ball, out of reach. Foot, leaping, twisting in midair (he must have heard me scream), knocked Ma to the pavement, his knee. . . . He let the ball go, which was not instinctive. Maybe that's as good as we got maybe.

The Sunday after the "60 Minutes" clip, during the last preseason game, the unexpected reared. Or perhaps the inevitable. In Foot's case, maybe the desired. I didn't say that.
After a completed field goal, Foot, *bouncing, bouncing, watching the ball sail over the catch net* . . . announcers going:

"Rose did not play college ball, but back in high school, which, judging by the gray hair coming out of his helmet, was some time ago" . . . *bouncing, bouncing, it almost seemed waiting for some name-hungry defensive back built low and heavy like a hog to come in and blindside him like a pin setter.*

And he did come. *A dark streak, low from the left, Foot's cleats gripping the artificial turf. Knee an explosion. The gun.*

Foot Rose would never play football again. That's what the doctors said. But on the basis of his knowledge of kicking technique and his short burst of media attention (so short you might have missed it), he was offered a position in China teaching soccer players how to address the ball. Later he became the first non-Russian football coach in the Soviet Union.

At least these are the rumors.

As a sign of bereavement which I now consider bizarre, I bought a cage full of pigeons from a kid and set them free in a kind of Olympic salute.

"Dreaming just comes natural," I said as I slid back the slat roof of the cage. Pigeons rushed past me in an explosion of white and gray, whirled once overtop of me, and returned to their box. Not even one tried to escape.

"What did they have her in?" Foot asked me on the day I left. We were in a seedy bar. He was wearing a stained brown trench coat, leaning on an umbrella for a cane, looking very much the wino.

"Running togs," I said.

"I thought so." Foot tipped his head, emptied his glass. He wiped his mouth with a sleeve, fixed his liquid eyes on me. "I figured you'd lie to save me."

Rumors

We need them like the young need sleep and we pass them around like drinks. We mow our busy lawns, watch sports off the satellite, and wait for it to happen. We deaden ourselves.

Once in a while a friend will ask for the story I am telling, and I'll do my best—though to be honest, it's hard. Sometimes Foot is toiling in an industrial semipro league somewhere in the northeast, sometimes we nearly make it on "Donahue." One time three adults scrimmaged in the street after dark. Usually I falter before the end because I don't know how to finish this story.

How do you explain youth slipping by?

$\mathcal{L}$IMBO RIVER

$\mathcal{T}$he bus trip took so long we felt like bugs trapped in a jar. It didn't seem like we were getting anywhere. The windows always framed the same rigid mountain wall, and the same highway unscrolled blackly before us like a river. I slept a lot. My mother awoke me as we passed Frank Slide, the horizon ruined by chunks of rock the size of houses.

"In the middle of the night," she whispered to me, "a mountain collapsed and buried the town that was here. There was only one survivor, a baby girl. Nobody knew anything about her, so they called her Frankie."

I pictured a mountain splintering like a rotten molar, a baby sitting in an ocean of rock and rubble. Rain was slanting into my window, making the same tinny sound as it had on the roof of our trailer back in Chilliwack. I pictured saucepans in the aisle catching the plink plink of falling rain.

"Nobody knew anything about her," my mother said. "Think about that. Total freedom!"

The first thing we set eyes on when the taxi dropped us off in front of the Alamo apartments was Marcel. He was sitting on one of three kitchen chairs set out on the lawn. The legs had been pounded into the ground like tent pegs so they wouldn't move, and the grass beneath them sprang up nearly to the seats. Even though it was about seventy-five degrees out, he had on a stained canvas parka with pockets huge enough to hide his beer bottle in.

My mother pretended to survey the area. Across the street was a park and a river that glistened like foil. The heads of some children bobbed offshore, and water-skiers slalomed around them, peeling off strips of brightness.

When it became clear Marcel wasn't going to help Mom with the two boxes of belongings she was carrying, she thumped them down on the sidewalk and lit a cigarette. When she was on the wagon she hated drinkers, but she chain-smoked.

Marcel said, "I don't blame them kids for playing hookey. School's just another prison."

Mom said flatly, "Kids belong in school."

"Why isn't he then?" Marcel was pointing at me.

"Good Lord, we just got into town." My mother looked down at Marcel. "Why aren't you at work?"

I thought he was sick; maybe that was why he had the parka on, but Marcel said simply: "I'm on welfare." And as if he read my thoughts: "This coat ain't warm as it looks."

My mother raised her chin as if about to sneeze, then patted down her skirt. "Unfortunately we are on welfare ourselves, but not for long. I think it damages the human spirit."

"Sure, but it beats working."

Mom was flabbergasted, "Work is what makes the world go around!"

"Work is prison," Marcel said, adding, "Give me welfare or give me death."

Her lips got hard as two bones. "Is that alcohol you're drinking out here in public?"

She knew darn well it was; she'd served enough of it in her day. But she was fed up, I could see it. This man perched on a kitchen chair on a lawn drinking beer in the middle of the afternoon had my numerous "uncles" written all over him. My mother had earned an aesthetician's diploma from beauty school, and wanted to make a fresh start away from the Marcels of this world. Problem was they were the only type of person who lived in the places we could afford.

"Is it?" she repeated.

"Why?" Marcel held the bottle out to her. "You want a swallow?"

"*Oh!*" Mom staggered inside with her boxes and Marcel said to me, "Who was that masked man?"

"Anita Sobchuck," I said. "She's my mother."

"Thank goodness," Marcel smiled, "for a minute there I thought she was mine."

Marcel swore he'd never done anything wrong in his lifetime. In fact the only reason he wound up in jail in the first place was for drunk driving.

"I drank for to get free," he told me, "and then I drove for to get free faster. Someday you'll know what I'm talking about." It was one of the few things Marcel ever told me that was true.

Crimped over street signs, squealed around corners up on two wheels, got into fenderbenders. Got his license taken away four times in six months, finally got a jail term.

"I went and nosed my car into a creek," he explained, sounding proud. "When the cops winched me out the next morning and made me blow, I *still* buried the needle!"

The pen was located out by where the blue vein of river wound through scrub prairie land. During exercise period, Marcel would hook his fingers through the chain link, look out over the river. It wasn't fair to be in there for just burning tire marks into lawns, etcetera, was it? Gusts of wind blew in off the river, pasted the hair to his head. The guards could tell he was shaking it rough, so they told an old con named Pope to go talk to him.

"Now the Pope," Marcel told me a few days after we'd moved into the Alamo, "was a recidivist criminal. B&Es, paperhanger, shanked a guard once . . . he'll die inside, but he's a smart cookie just the same. What he told me was to relax and roll with the punches.

"*'But I didn't do nothing wrong though,'* I told him. '*I don't even belong here!*'

"'You and me both, pal.' Pope slapped me on the back and said we were here for a good time, not a long time."

Marcel and me were sitting on the chairs pounded into the lawn, watching the river. Marcel said he liked to watch it because every day was a different river. The current worked like a knife. Ghostly sandbars rose out of the water, and each night the current would rearrange them, carve them away, or sometimes build on long spines of silt.

"Here's what the Pope really said," Marcel told me, "and I pass it on to you, Sean, for your wisdom bank: 'Society don't like you and has kicked you out. That's why you're here. Take a look around,' he said, 'these ain't the first walls you been inside—'"

I looked over my shoulder at the Alamo, then back out at the river.

"'Get wise,' he told me, 'roll with the punches.' I'll never forget him telling me that."

My mom didn't like me hanging around with Marcel, but what else was there to do? Most of the other tenants were at the bar by the time I got home from school, and we didn't have a TV. For a while I swam in the river with the other kids, but then Mom found out they were metis and forbade it.

"Why?"

"They're half-breeds."

"So?"

"Ringworm, rickets, head lice," she said.

So it was me and Marcel. He told me "Limbo is good for the body and what's good for the body is good for the soul." Same went for smokey sausages, Player's sailor-cut cigarettes, whiskey, beer, and wine. He said, "In the old days when limbo was big and competitions were held all across the country, and the prizes were booze, nobody bought liquor when Marcel Gebege was in town."

And he limboed for me once in a while. Put a yardstick across the mouths of two forty-ounce whiskey bottles, spread his feet wide, and crab-walked underneath, hopping on the bolts of his ankles. I was only eight or nine at the time, and could bend like a pipe cleaner, but I couldn't get as low as Marcel. He got snakebelly low.

He told me how a cell is a bowl about the size of an empty head. That's how teeny his thinking got in jail. He said, "In jail, time is slow and quiet as a bowl of water. If you look into it you can see things. For instance, I sense your Mom doesn't really like me, does she?"

"I guess not."

"That's OK. Most people don't. Do you like me, Sean?"

"Yes."

"I thought you would. You remind me of myself at your age. A bit of a loner."

The reason Marcel drank at home instead of in one of the bars across the river was because he was having an affair with the woman who lived across the hall from him, Rhonda Bighead. I already knew plenty about hanky-panky, so it didn't take long to figure it out. When Rhonda's old man would go to the bar, Marcel would watch until he was on the far side of the bridge, then he'd peel his rear end off his kitchen chair and say: "Excuse me, I think I'll repair to my place for a nap."

Rhonda's old man's name was Ralph. He had arm muscles like big baloney rolls and his teeth were all punched out from bar brawls.

Mom was furious when she learned about Marcel and Rhonda. She was having a lot of trouble finding a job as an aesthetician and was smoking more than ever, which cost money.

"That bitch is using him!" she cried at me one night. Mom had gone down to the laundry room and saw Marcel's phone cord snaking out from under his door, across the hall carpet, disappearing under Rhonda's.

"She's just after him for his phone!" Mom insisted. I think she was jealous for not getting the idea first. Plus Marcel wasn't a bad catch. He was about fifty-five but he looked forty and seemed quite healthy for drinking all the time.

We didn't have a phone ourselves because we couldn't afford the deposit yet, and this made it hard for Mom to fill out applications for work. Another thing was, we didn't know anybody, and sometimes we felt stranded without a phone. It made Mom's blood boil to think of that slut Rhonda Bighead having a heart-to-heart with somebody on Marcel's phone when we didn't have a phone to use, or a soul to call up even if we did.

The river started to drop. In some places it looked more like a highway than a river. Marcel told me when the ice goes off a river, it makes a sound like somebody standing behind a hill with a handgun.

"One of the stupidest things I ever did," Marcel told me, "was try to escape from the pen. I climbed the fence in the night and found myself on the river ice. It was April and the ice was breaking. It started to crack up and I was leaping floe to floe, ice swirling all around me like broken bottles of rye. I could have gone under at any time, the ice would have closed over me, and I would have drowned. But I'm lucky that way. I just keep pulling up aces. What's the stupidest thing you've done so far?"

I had taken money from my mom's purse and had shoplifted, but before I could answer, Marcel said, "Too many to pick from, huh? Well, let me tell you about the lowest I ever got. You got a minute?"

"Yes."

"Okay, listen and you might learn something. This was up in Fort Steele where I was working—last job I ever had. Anyways, one night I get this phone call. Come to Vancouver right away. Your son's been scalded. He was about two or three years old at the time. He'd be about your age now, I guess. Anyway, his mother'd put him in the tub to sleep and somehow he turned on the tap and scalded himself and drowned—"

He looked at me and wiped his mouth.

"—What was I supposed to do? I went to the airport, but they said: no seats left. *Lookit!*—I need to get back for my little boy's funeral *tomorrow!* Don't raise your voice at me, the ticket woman said, what a bitch. Anyways, so I go into the little lounge they got there at the airport, and I'm telling this story to the bartender when this lady at the bar—a real good looker, kind of looked like your mom—says I can have her seat.

"About two minutes later an announcement comes over the loudspeaker: *Seats available on flight to Vancouver, seats available.* So I don't need her ticket, but I'll be damned if me and this woman don't end up sitting beside each other on the flight. We have a few drinks, and when we land in Vancouver we go to a bar in Gastown, a real nice place. Anyways, we're not there half an hour when a brawl starts and I'm sucked into it. When the cops come to bust it up, they check my ID and it turns out I got a warrant out on me for not paying alimony, so they take me downtown and lock me up. Next morning I'm up before the judge. I say, 'Your honor, sir, I am a few months behind in alimony—true—but I have come for my little boy's funeral, and I have money to cover the alimony.' The judge looks at me for a minute. Then he says: *'Release this man.* He should *never* have spent the night in jail. Take him out right now, and when he hits the front doors: *immediate release!'*"

"Immediate release," I repeated dumbly. I wondered about the boy. Did he turn on the tap with his toes, or what?

"That's the kind of guy I am," Marcel said. "Lucky."

One night after school, I was in the laundry room folding shirts when I heard Ralph's voice booming through the wall.

"What do you care?" Rhonda screeched in return. "Marcel is your friend, too!"

Holy shit. I pressed my ear against the wall. Furniture was sliding across the floor, dishes shattering. I recognized the sound of somebody being thrown around and slapped the way Mom sometimes hit me for doing things that bugged her. She never meant to do it, but she got frustrated with my behavior sometimes. Later she would cry about it and say, "Let's forget that ever happened, OK Sean?" Sniffing back tears, hugging me. "Let's start fresh, OK honey?" And we would. For a while things would be fine, but it always happened again. So what?—I knew my mother loved me and never meant to hurt me.

I heard a terrible scream, then nothing.

It scared me so I ran upstairs, but I knew Mom wouldn't be home. I sat for a minute in the quiet apartment, then descended the steps and knocked on Rhonda's door.

"What do you want?" Ralph barked.

"This is Sean from upstairs?"

"You better come in here, man."

Rhonda's arm had been opened up with a butcher knife. Also her back from when she must have tried to get out the door. She was laying on her side on the floor, eyelids flickering like she'd been woken up and was trying to get back to sleep. I tried to back out the door, but Ralph started crying.

"What was I supposed to do?" he pleaded. "I love her." He was sitting on the couch staring into space. "You better call Diamond Cab." He pointed at Marcel's phone, on the carpet just inside the door.

They were piling into the cab to take Rhonda to the hospital when two police cruisers closed in front of the Alamo, cherries pulsing the dark river. Somebody else must have phoned them and there they were, cuffing Ralph, pushing him by the head into the back seat.

An ambulance blinked up and one of the attendants got out and snapped down the legs on a gurney. "Where's the victim at?"

A tall cop said, "What victim? The victim of history and circumstance or the one he just carved up?" He laughed.

Rhonda wheeled around, bandage on her arm bright. "Don't you fuck dare talk about him!"

In the rear of the cruiser, Ralph was swimming back and forth across the dark blue cage, slamming the windows, the wire mesh.

Marcel immersed himself in booze. He drank like a man taking off his clothes and getting into a pool of water. Floating the way a heart floats in a chest. That's how depressed he was.

"Rhonda's cut me off," he said to me, "but I still let her use my phone. What the hell. Know what I mean, Sean?"

"Kind of, I guess."

"Well if you don't, you will soon enough. You know what I just noticed about you?" Marcel said. "You're kind of quiet the way I was when I was a kid."

I never felt quiet. I just thought nobody ever listened to me.

"I'll tell you something you probably won't believe, but when I was your age—and this is just between you and me, OK?—I had a club foot that since has been repaired by surgery. Would you believe I spent every recess of my school life over by the playground fence, looking out at the street so I wouldn't get a soccer ball bounced off my face?"

"Really?"

"Absolutely." He patted his chest with the palms of his hands. "And look at me now. The sky's the limit. You'll see."

A few days later Marcel presented me with a bike, an expensive BMX. It wasn't new, but Marcel said it was even better than new since it had already been broken in. He'd found it in the river and used a solution to clean off the rust.

He said he was crossing the bridge on his way to the Shamrock bar when he caught something glittering in one of the pools. He couldn't believe it: a bicycle, the chrome rims glinting like a pair of eye glasses.

Maybe somebody stole it and threw it off the bridge when the water was high. Or maybe it happened during winter and had spent months on the ice covered in snow. Poor people were always going out onto the ice and falling through. They fell through cracks and were swept away by the current, never to be heard from again. The mounties didn't even bother to look for them until spring when they could drag the river. By then the victims were misshapen balloons hung up in debris after spending all winter locked in their frozen bodies under the ice.

That night, on his way home from the Shamrock, Marcel stumbled down to the river, over the sandbars, and waded the shallow water to the pool. He stripped off his shirt and pants and slipped in. He said he felt superhuman: doing it for me because a boy my age should have a bike.

He floated on the surface, looking down at the round lenses of the wheels. That's when he saw them—blue shapes darting, flashing in the blackness.

"Fish," Marcel told Mom and me, "maybe half a dozen of them. Big bottom feeders—carp or suckers. Maybe even sturgeon—"

I pictured shadowy blades hovering above the bicycle, facing into the slow current, mouths sucking up food.

"But the river's drying up," Mom said as Marcel oiled the chain of my BMX. "The water's so shallow—" she looked at the river, one hand in a salute against the sunset. "How are they supposed to get out?"

"They aren't," Marcel said. "That's the whole idea. It's nature's way."

The metis kids climbed up out of the river and crossed the park to ride my bike. They couldn't do it any better than me though. I guess they'd never had a bike before either. They wobbled up and down the street in front of the Alamo, weaving in and out of traffic until my mom put her foot down. She hated them and made me understand we weren't like them, we weren't.

A few nights later I was entertaining myself by tightrope walking the rim of the fence that separated the Alamo from the chrome-and-glass condo next door when Mom clicked up the sidewalk in her high-heeled shoes. She brushed off the seat of a kitchen chair and sat down next to Marcel.

"You'll be pleased to know, Sean, that I begin work tomorrow at Beauty City—"

"Congratulations, Anita," Marcel said. "That calls for a toast." He hoisted his beer bottle into the air.

"Thank you, Mister Gebege." Mom took out a cigarette and Marcel held his lighter under it. "I see you are still supporting the breweries."

Marcel squinted: "Listen, I drink for to get free."

"No doubt," Mom laughed, adding that she had spent too many years working in the bar industry not to recognize a man living his life out of a bottle when she saw one.

Marcel looked wounded.

"I'm teasing," Mom said, smiling, blowing smoke out of her nostrils. I could tell she was feeling high, excited about the future. "Thank you again," she said, "for Sean's bike."

It was chained to the fence. In the dark it looked like a pair of sunglasses. I wasn't allowed to ride at night, but after school I loved to pedal through the streets above the Alamo. Some of the richest old homes in town were up there—pillared porches, yards full of big trees. As I sped by them it seemed likely that Mom and me would end up in one of those places. Good luck was just around the corner. At dusk I would ride home, following the gravel alley that descended steeply to the river. The yards on top had green swimming pools, but these quickly gave way to overgrown vegetation and broken-down cars. The yards near the bottom were hidden behind rickety unpainted fences, and big dogs threw themselves into the boards, barking loudly as I passed.

Marcel offered Mom a beer and this time she took it. "What

the heck?" she said, and held it out as if toasting the river. "To new beginnings," though it was the same old beginning, same old snowball starting to roll.

"Don't look at me like that, Sean, I'm just celebrating. Can't I do that?"

"Your mother is allowed to have some fun too, isn't she, big guy?" Marcel punched me lightly on the shoulder and Mom giggled.

Somehow at that moment I knew I was in for another uncle. Which meant I would be losing both my mother and only friend in one fell swoop, but at least we'd have a phone.

I looked away, up at the flat purple streak above the river. I had patches on the knees of my pants and oversized Sally Ann runners on my feet. I started to feel sorry for myself, but then I thought of my bike, and my spirits soared a bit.

Every day a different river. The water kept dropping until parts of it shrunk to a thin trickle like an overflowing sink. The skiers and kids moved upriver where the current still gouged the channel deep. In front of the Alamo, sandbars started to sprout grass.

A couple of days after Mom started making me call Marcel "Uncle Marcel," Ralph came to the door, slapping the fat end of a baseball bat into the palm of his hand. Rhonda wouldn't press charges, so he was on the street again.

"Where's Marcel, and no bullshit, OK? I got nothing against you, man, but I know your old lady's got a key to his place, and if you don't let me into it I'm going to have to club you." Even though I was only eight, he waved the bat in my face. I doubt he would have done anything to me, but I let him into Marcel's anyway. For a lot of reasons it seemed like the right thing to do.

Marcel wasn't in his apartment so Ralph commenced to smash things up. Caved in the aquarium so water gushed onto the carpet, then ground his heels on the little fish that flipped around on the floor. Punched a few holes in the gyprock. Brought the bat down over the top of the TV so the tube exploded across the carpet. He placed a few long-distance calls on the telephone, then hung up and splintered it with the bat.

137

Then he tucked Marcel's toaster oven under his arm and left.

Marcel was sitting on our couch shaking when I got back upstairs.

"Did he at least leave me one beer?"

"You're lucky he didn't find you. He wanted to break your knees."

"Fuck him if he can't take a joke," Marcel said, grinning. Then he shook his head in amazement. "But you're right, I'm lucky. I just keep pulling up aces."

One of the metis kids drowned in the river, went down as if a weight was attached to his ankles.

A friend dove and dove for him, surfacing to fill his lungs, shaking his head. A grainy photo in the newspaper had the spray from his hair making a white flower on the water.

The mounties launched a small boat, dragged a grappling hook back and forth across the river. The water-skiers spiraled the area in their boat and a boy not much older than me sat on the prow, stabbing a paddle into the water.

The drowned boy's friends collapsed on shore, crying in disbelief. They had been swimming to the sandbar where the skiers partied, but they didn't make it. Their hands clutched the sand, their feet were in the river.

A few mornings later I went downstairs to go to school and found my BMX missing. I couldn't believe it. I thought I must have left it somewhere, but I knew I hadn't, and my next thought was, those fucking half-breeds had stolen it. Mom was right about them. All day in school I steamed. I pictured them climbing out of the water like mutant swamp monsters, taking what was mine. I almost totally forgot about the drowning. How could those hooky-playing sonofabitches steal my bike after I let them use it?

When I got home Uncle Marcel was sitting on one of the chairs. By now the grass was so long it draped over his lap like a luau skirt. He was pickled out of his mind.

"I have to show you something," he said.

"What?" I looked around excited, thinking he'd found my bike.

Marcel said, "Right there in front of you. The car." An old, bald-tired clunker was parked at the curb. "A friend owed me a favor so I got this off him for fifty bucks. What a steal, hey, Sean?"

A whistling started in my ears and I backed away. "You stole my bike," I said. *"Didn't you?"* The idea just flashed in my mind.

"Hey, you hold on! I didn't steal anything."

I glared at him. That bike was the best thing that ever happened to me. It was more than transportation, it *transported me,* changed the way I saw myself. When I was on it, skimming the streets, everything was possible. And now Marcel had taken it back.

"I didn't steal anything. It was my bike," Marcel said. "I found it and I let you use it and then I took it back. Actually I found the original owner and returned it to him."

"Liar!" I cried. I couldn't help it. Huge, wracking sobs shook my lungs and I thought I was going to drown from lack of air.

When Mom came home, she stormed into my room. "I told you to keep that damn bike locked!" Her breath smelled of booze. "If you don't look after your things you don't deserve them!"

"I did lock it! Marcel stole it!"

"Shut your dirty lying mouth!" my mom screamed at me, bringing her hand back to slap.

Though it wasn't mentioned in so many words, I'm sure it was partly due to the bike episode, to smooth things over, that we went to the fair. Also, Marcel hadn't taken the clunker anywhere yet and wanted to feel the road beneath him. For my part I'd never seen a circus, zoo, marine world, or wax museum, much less a fair, and though I hated the idea of being bribed into being nice and civil again, I really wanted to go.

As we were pulling away, Rhonda Bighead and Ralph were reeling through the park on the way home from the Shamrock. Rhonda's gashes had healed nicely and she was holding a bouquet of white flowers Ralph had torn from a bed in the park. When they came to a patch of red flowers, he bent like a hero and ripped out a whole plant.. Rhonda hugged it to her, roots dripping dirt. Then she lost her balance, staggered a few steps, and pitched over. Ralph tried to help her up, but toppled onto her, at which point she started yelling, slapping him on the head.

Marcel spewed some beer out of his nostrils, and Mom eyed him. She didn't mind him drinking, but drinking and driving didn't mix.

Marcel tooted the horn as we passed and Rhonda turned, cursing us, hurling flowers.

The clunker had a shot transmission, so we had to stop about every thirty miles for Marcel to add fluid. This was synchronized perfectly with his need to stop and water the ditch. It got dark and the pavement glistened like ice on a frozen river. For miles, it seemed, I could see the yellow Ferris wheel lights shining in the sky, and despite everything I got so excited I thought I could smell foot longs, corn dogs, and candy apples over the cigarette smoke in the car.

It was a bottom-of-the-barrel fair. Workers all tattooed up like a bad face; rides greasy, probably suffering from metal fatigue. The foot longs were about the length of your thumb and cost two bucks each. But so what? It was a fair! And the night was swept along in a blur of light and color, odor, sound.

Mom and Marcel rode the Death Trap, a bench chained to a giant arm that whirled around in the air like a propeller. Me, I flopped a rubber frog onto a lily pad with a huge tongue depressor and won a fly in a cube of clear plastic. Marcel limboed under a wooden rod set on bowling pins—passed through like he was kneeling on air—and won a stuffed snake he gave to Mom. Mom won a plaster sea gull for stumping the Guesser on what exactly she did at Beauty City.

"Hey boy," the Guesser said to me as we were leaving his booth, "I bet I know what you want to be when you grow up." A crowd of people had gathered to watch him perform, but nobody was investing in his act, so he was using me to drum up business. "Most kids want to be the same as their dad," he said. "It's genetic."

The crowd chuckled.

"Are you proud of your old dad?" The Guesser answered himself. "I bet you are." All the time his eyes were hunting the crowd for my father, a clue to my future. "Is your dad here with you?" he said finally.

I never knew my real father, but had no reason to suspect he would be any different from Marcel, so that's who I pointed at. The crowd turned to him and the smile dropped off Marcel's face. He looked down at his feet. For the first time I saw the guilt and shame that was probably always there, under the surface of the stories and drunken sprees. Marcel was King of the Alamo Apartments, but in the world of upright citizens he was just a drunken bum. That's what the murmuring crowd saw and I didn't blame them. How else could you judge the bulbous red nose, the gaps in his teeth, the creased map of his face?

Even the Guesser momentarily lost his composure, but he quickly regained it. "Kids like their teachers," he said, winking at me. "I bet you want to be a schoolteacher." This surprised me. I expected doctor or fireman. "But," the Guesser added, taking a plaster ornament off his shelf, "I'm not always a hundred percent right on, so here—" He offered me the ornament.

I glanced at Marcel who was still looking down. "No," I said, "you're right, I do want to be a teacher."

I refused the ornament, but the Guesser forced me to take it anyway, as though he didn't believe me. It was a figurine of a pointy-headed troll.

When we got away from there Marcel put one arm over my shoulder, the other over Mom's and said, "A teacher? Well why the hell not?" We all laughed.

Who knows what anybody is going to become? Maybe at one time Marcel envisioned something different for himself, but now life was just a river he was being swept down, and he was happy. My mother believed we could alter the course of our lives if we were strong and lucky enough, and if we had faith. One out of three isn't bad. In a way I think they were both right: nobody gets what they deserve, but in the end we all become who we want to be, deep down. I don't know.

At about midnight Marcel took me onto the Zipper.

It was a mesh cage that spun and orbited around a greasy hub like a planet around a star. There were broken bolts and nuts in the popcorn and cigarette butts scattered around the base, but we didn't care. "We're here for a good time, not a long time," Marcel laughed. And as he said this our cage jerked, lifted us into the night sky, and we spun upside down, and Marcel's change flew out of his pockets, whizzed past our ears like shrapnel. My heart tore free of my chest and I felt it in my mouth. We dove toward the ground, but at the last minute were scooped up, swirling through the blackness, me and Marcel, screaming at the stars between our shoes.

Previous Winners of the
DRUE HEINZ LITERATURE PRIZE

The Death of Descartes
David Bosworth
1981

Dancing for Men
Robley Wilson, Jr.
1982

Private Parties
Jonathan Penner
1983

The Luckiest Man in the World
Randall Silvis
1984

The Man Who Loved Levittown
W. D. Wetherell
1985

Under the Wheat
Rick DeMarinis
1986

In the Music Library
Ellen Hunnicutt
1987

Moustapha's Eclipse
Reginald McKnight
1988

Cartographies
Maya Sonenberg
1989